Murder in the Choir Room

Murder in the Choir Room

Stephen E. Stanley

Author's Note:

Anyone familiar with Bath, Maine will realize that I have taken great liberties with the geography and history of the town. There is no All Souls Church. I have used the historic Winter Street Church as the setting, though it is no longer an active place of worship.

This book is a work of fiction. All characters, names, institutions, and situations depicted in the book are the product of my imagination and not based on any persons living or dead. Anyone who thinks he or she is depicted in the book probably needs to get a life.

Stonefield Publishing
Portland, Maine
Stonefieldpublishing@gmail.com

Author's web page: www.stephenestanley.com

"The language of friendship is not words but meanings."
–Henry David Thoreau

Chapter 1

It was the first Sunday after Labor Day and the church was packed. I was sitting in the choir stalls with the rest of the tenors and basses. The women were sitting in front of us, and we had just finished singing the anthem. I was really trying hard to pay attention, but all I could think about was the Colonel's secret fried chicken recipe and a side of mashed potatoes and gravy. I find it hard to be holy when I'm hungry.

This Sunday was Homecoming Sunday and both the church school and the choir were in session for the first time after the summer break. Apparently God had taken the summer off because there had been no Sunday school and no choir since late May. Each summer most of the churches around here change their services from ten o'clock to nine o'clock, except for the Unitarians who cancel church altogether. I was pretty sure from reading the morning newspapers that this wasn't a good time for God to go on vacation.

The organ postlude ended and people began to file out of the church. I was at the back of the line as the choir made its way to the choir room. I could see the flutter of burgundy choir robes in front of me as we filed out of the sanctuary and through the narrow hallway toward the choir room. I was in the process of unbuttoning my robe when I heard a scream and the fluttering choir robes were suddenly still. I ran down the hallway and pushed through the group of singers to see what had caused the commotion.

"Someone call 911," I said to the group, but I could see that the body on the floor was well past the services of the EMTs.

"Everybody out of the room. Nobody touch anything!" Tim Mallory, the police chief, had been waiting for me, heard the scream, and came to investigate. Nobody had moved; everyone seemed to be in shock. "Now!" yelled Tim, and the choir members began to disperse.

The body was lying on its side with a small pool of blood on the floor where someone had bashed in his skull. Several of the choir chairs had been overturned and but there was nothing in view that looked like the murder weapon. Even so it was very clear that this was no accident.

"Jesse, do you recognize him at all?" Tim asked me.

I looked at the body but couldn't tell much from the doorway where I was standing. Suppressing a shudder, I entered the choir room, knelt down, and took a closer look.

"It's Jack Riley," I answered. Jack was the head trustee of the church, a local school board member. And not to speak ill of the dead, but he was a general pain in the ass as well.

"That's what I thought, too." Tim said to me.

There was no breeze in the air, and it was hot and stuffy for a

September afternoon. I sat on the front porch sipping a gin and tonic and waited for Tim to come home. Tim is my...well, it's hard to describe. Partner, sounds too much like a business arrangement, and boyfriend sounds too juvenile and heterosexual, but you get the general idea.

Tim had radioed for backup and I knew that most of All Souls Church was probably cordoned off with yellow crime tape. An officer had taken down everyone's statements and sent us on our way. There was nothing for me to do now but wait. Whatever happened, it wasn't going to be good for the church or the community.

My dog Argus had a perfectly comfortable bed on the porch next to my rocking chair, but like most pugs, he preferred my lap and was happily napping while I was rocking. A car pulled onto the street and Argus pricked up his ears. Dogs have amazing hearing and can tell the sound of one car from another. Argus's tail started to wag as Rhonda Shepard parked her car and came up the walkway. I gave Rhonda a wave and left Argus to greet her while I went into the kitchen to make her a gin and tonic. Rhonda had a flare for vintage clothing and hair styles. Today she was wearing a 1930s black dress with big buttons down the front. Her hair was in a bun. She looked like the president of the Ladies' Temperance Society.

"You might need this," I said to Rhonda as I passed her the drink. She was sitting on one of the rockers with Argus in her lap. Rhonda and I had both taught English in the same New Hampshire school for over thirty years. When she opened her business in Bath, Maine, I decided to follow her here and help out.

"I missed most of the excitement. The congregation had left the church before the police got there," she said. I told her what I had seen and heard and she just nodded her head.

"This is a pretty small town and I'm sure Tim will get it solved in no time," I said. I wasn't so sure though.

"I've read that most murders are committed by close friends or family members," said Rhonda between sips of gin and tonic.

"If Jack Riley had any close friends I'd like to meet them." Maybe I was being too harsh.

"He did seem to make a few enemies, like every teacher and parent in the school district for example."

"Not to mention every committee member of All Souls Church," I added.

"He was usually right about money matters and had a good head for figures," Rhonda replied. "It was the way he put down everyone who didn't agree with him that made him unpopular."

"Still, calling someone a silly fool in public, harsh as that is, is no motive for murder."

"No chance it was an accident?" Rhonda asked.

"He was face down, head turned to the side, and the back of his head was bashed in. He must have died quickly, because there was very little blood."

Rhonda passed her empty glass to me. "Make the

next one a double."

"Good idea," I replied.

Rhonda and I were on our second round of gin and tonics when a red SUV drove up the street and the Reverend Mary Bailey got out of the driver's side and headed up the walk. Sixty and usually jovial, Mary Bailey had a tragic look on her face.

"This has been a most heartbreaking day," she said as she took a seat on the porch.

"Can I get you something to drink?" I asked as I held up my gin and tonic.

"How about a cup of herb tea?"

"You got it! I'll be right back," I replied as I headed to the kitchen.

When I returned with the tea, Mary had her glasses off and was wiping her eyes. As a caring pastor, Mary would be called on to minister to a congregation in shock.

"I just spent the last hour with Jack Riley's family," began Mary. "They are devastated as you can imagine. The police are questioning them now, so I thought I would check in with all you choir members since you people were the first to find the body. I'm sure you're all upset. I wanted to start here first to see if you had any news from Tim."

"No, I haven't heard anything from Tim. I'm sure as soon as he can he'll let me know."

"How are you doing, Mary?" asked Rhonda. "It must be very difficult for you."

Stephen E. Stanley

"Oh, yes. A death in the congregation is always a difficult thing, but this..." Tears welled up in Mary's eyes. Rhonda and I wanted to offer comfort, but there wasn't much to say.

Chapter 2

The September sunset was spectacular as Rhonda and I watched the day slipping away. Neither of us felt like being alone so Rhonda agreed to stay for supper. I had no idea when Tim would show up, but I suspected he would be late. I didn't feel much like cooking so I grabbed a package out of the freezer and set it on the counter. Finally a breeze began to stir outside, and the curtains in the windows began to flutter with the fresh air.

"How about if I thaw out some beef burgundy?" I asked Rhonda.

"Sounds good to me," she replied.

Argus was underfoot as I put the frozen packages in the microwave. The dog was, of course, hoping something would drop on the floor, when suddenly he lifted up his ears and ran for the door. It was a sure sign that Tim had just driven up the driveway.

"What a fucking bad day!" bemoaned Tim as he came into the kitchen with Argus leading the way. Tim took a seat at the table, and I started mixing gin and tonics for all of us. Tim was still in his Sunday church clothes, and they were looking a little worse for wear. I rarely drink more than one drink, but then I rarely see murdered bodies in churches, so we all had a round of drinks. The three of us sat in silence for a few minutes.

"Well?" I asked Tim after we sat there for a while.

"There isn't much to tell. The techs have been all over the place, but we haven't found a weapon or any evidence yet. And we don't have a motive. The family is distraught, as you can imagine, and not very helpful at this point, and nobody at church saw anything unusual."

The microwave beeped and I took out the beef burgundy and dished it out into three bowls. I grabbed a loaf of bread and put it on the table with the bowls.

"Sorry, it's just leftovers," I said. "But it really wasn't a cooking day."

"This is great," said Tim. "I haven't had anything to eat all day."

"Better than anything I have at home," added Rhonda. We ate in silence for a while.

"What was Jack doing in the choir room? He wasn't in the choir," I asked. I couldn't stand the silence much longer.

"That's a good question," answered Tim. "We found the pouch with the morning's collection after we moved the body. It was under him. It doesn't appear that robbery was a motive, because as near as we can tell, all the money is there."

"What was he doing with the collection?" asked Rhonda.

"After the collection is taken, the ushers in the back of the church put the money in a pouch, place it in an offering plate, and bring it to the front of the church during the singing of the doxology. Then one of the trustees of the church takes it to the church office and places it in the safe," I explained.

"The church office is in the opposite direction from the choir room," Rhonda observed.

"Yes, it is," said Tim.

"It's a church; nothing is locked on a Sunday," I added.

"But there are people all around," said Rhonda.

"And so far, nobody saw anything unusual," concluded Tim.

"I think people are just a little shaken up at the news. Maybe in a few days they will start to remember something. We can maybe find something out when we talk to them later," I said.

Tim looked at me carefully. "*We* are not going to do any such thing. The last time I looked, you were not on the police force," Tim said to me, but not unkindly.

"Whatever!" I smiled innocently.

"Well," began Rhonda, "I should get along home now."

"Me, too," sighed Tim. "I need to shower and get some fresh clothes for tomorrow morning. I'll pick you up for lunch tomorrow," he said to me.

The sun was rising later and later each day as the summer was slowly morphing into autumn. After a quick and unhealthy breakfast, I harnessed up Argus and we headed out the door. Argus was always happy to go anywhere, so we headed off to town.

All Souls Parish Church is a typical New England

white colonial church structure. Its beauty is in its simplicity and scale. It sits on High Street facing the city park and the library, its steeple can be seen from across the river.

As Argus and I approached the church, I noticed Mary Bailey's SUV in the driveway and decided to stop in at her office to see how she was doing. Argus always hesitates at unfamiliar doorways, and he gave the threshold a sniff just to make sure it was not a vet's office. Assured that it wasn't, he led the way down the hall. Mary looked up as I knocked on the door, and I could tell she had been crying.

"Jesse Ashworth!" exclaimed Mary, "I'm glad you stopped by. Hi Argus!" she leaned over to pat the dog. Argus jumped in her lap and started licking her face.

"I hope you like dogs," I said.

"Oh, yes," she said and started to laugh. Argus seemed to have that effect on people. She indicated that I should sit down. I noticed that the lights on the phone were flashing.

"I'll bet the reporters have been calling you all morning," I said.

"The answer machine was full when I walked in the door. I'm waiting for Delores to come in and go through them for me." Delores is the church's administrative assistant. "I'm working on an official statement for the media now. But I'm really having a hard time writing it."

"Just make it brief," I suggested. "'Our prayers are with the family at this tragic time.' That type of thing. Let Tim as police chief give the more detailed statements."

"I know," she sighed. "It's just that it's all so difficult. I don't know where to start."

"Did you notice anything unusual yesterday?" I asked by way of changing the subject. "You get to face the congregation for most of the service."

"Nothing unusual. The front doors of the church were open because of the stuffy weather. There were people walking by on the sidewalk, but that's not unusual. Did you see anything from the choir?" she asked.

"No, but my view of the congregation is somewhat blocked by the pulpit." I replied. "Was there anything unusual about the service itself? Did Jack Riley always pick up the collection?"

"The trustees take turns picking up the collections. They have a schedule of duties." Mary looked thoughtful for a moment. "He wasn't scheduled for the collection yesterday." She was looking puzzled as well.

"And?" I asked.

"And," she added. "The trustees usually wait until the end of the service to take the collection. Jack took the collection away before the end of the service."

I left Mary to write her official statement, and Argus and I continued on our way to work. Three mornings a week I work at Erebus, which is the name of Rhonda's gift shop. I handle the Internet sales, which of late were doing very well. In the last year the store inventory had changes from plastic lobsters and ceramic lighthouses to Maine handicrafts and some New Age items. Crystals, Tarot cards, and Ouija boards were selling quite well, despite, or maybe because of the downturn in the economy.

"Good morning'" said Rhonda as I came through the door. Today she was wearing a polyester pant suit from the 1970's with her hair hanging loose. I filled her in on my morning meeting with Pastor Mary.

"The poor thing," observed Rhonda. "She's left to deal with the emotional mess of this, isn't she?"

"I'm afraid so," I answered.

"Well, she is probably better equipped than any of us. Still I wouldn't want her job for anything."

"Slow day?" I asked, looking around at the empty store.

"Mondays are usually slow, though it may pick up."

"Well, I should get to work; Mondays are the busiest day for Internet sales."

I went into the back office and seated myself behind the computer. Argus took his place under the desk and promptly went to sleep. Sure enough there was a list of orders that had come in over the weekend. It would take me most of the morning to process them.

I lost all track of time as I was working on the orders. Suddenly a shadow fell over my desk, and I looked up to see Tim standing in the doorway. At six foot four with a muscular frame, Tim pretty much fills up a doorway. He was wearing his starched white police chief uniform shirt.

The chiseled face, the broad shoulders and perfect smile made him look like a movie star cop. There is always something about a man in uniform!

"I hope that's not a gun you're hiding in there," I said as I looked up.

"That's not a gun," said Tim as he held out a bag with sandwiches and chips. Tim pulled a chair up to my desk, and I poured us both a cup of coffee from the coffee pot. I told him about my visit with Mary Bailey.

"So," Tim said by way of focusing on my news, "Jack Riley was not the scheduled trustee for the collection pick up?"

"That's correct."

"And he took the collection out of the sanctuary before the end of the service?"

"Yes," I answered. "Do you think it means anything?"

"It might. But probably not."

"Thanks for clarifying," I responded.

"It's what I do," said Tim with a wink.

"So have you learned anything in your investigation?" I asked.

"The crime lab guys are going over everything, and an autopsy is scheduled for this afternoon. Unofficially, it looks like trauma to the head. We don't have a weapon identified yet. I have two detectives out questioning church members now, and the TV crews have already been here this morning."

"Busy twenty-four hours," I said.

"You got that right," answered Tim.

We made plans to spend the evening together and then Tim returned to work. After he left, Rhonda poked her head in.

"Could you watch the front?" she asked. "Jackson is taking me out to lunch." Jackson Bennett owned an insurance agency in town and has been the man in Rhonda's life for the past year.

"No problem," I answered. "So where are you eating?"

"Who said anything thing eating?" replied Rhonda as she giggled and took Jackson's arm. Yikes!

Chapter 3

The weather had turned cold by the time Rhonda returned, and it looked like it might rain later. Weather in New England is unpredictable in the in-between seasons of spring and fall. I harnessed up Argus, and we headed home. We walked down Front Street, up by the library and the park, and on up Winter Street passing by the church. I noticed that Mary Bailey's vehicle was gone and figured that she was probably ministering to Jack Riley's family. Jack had a wife and two grown children. I liked the wife, but had never met the children.

Heading up Sagamore Street, I passed by John and Dorothy Lowell's house. My elderly neighbors were nowhere in sight. My house was at the end of the street. It was a yellow 1920's bungalow that I had restored the previous year. A small sign on the front porch carried the name 'Eagle's Nest.' The sign came with the house, and it seemed to fit for some reason, so I kept the sign and the name.

The house was chilly, but I couldn't bring myself to turn on central heat this early in September; instead I built a fire in the living room to take off the chill. Then I busied myself in the kitchen making a pot of chili. I was currently experimenting with vegetarian recipes and planning to write a new cookbook. Several months ago I wrote a cookbook on comfort food. It had sold well, and while it didn't make me rich, it did give me a little spending money. Rhonda's sister, Janet, is a book agent in New York, and she found me a small niche publisher, and they send me a modest royalty check and four times a year.

Tim liked everything I cooked, and he hadn't seemed to notice that some of his meals were missing animal parts.

Argus, as always, was in the kitchen under my feet, hoping I would drop something on the floor. Every once in a while I did something clumsy and he got a carrot top or a potato chip. Suddenly Argus stopped in his tracks and bolted for the front door barking all the way. I knew Tim had just arrived.

"Smells good," said Tim as he poked his head into the kitchen. He was still dressed in his uniform. "Let me go change and I'll fix us some drinks."

"How about a nice cosmopolitan?" I asked.

"You got it."

Tim returned wearing a sweat suit and began making the drinks. My kitchen is small for two people to work in together, so we kept bumping into each other. Not really a bad thing, but it does slow things down a bit. Tim poured the drinks, and I put the cornbread into the oven, and we both sat down at the kitchen table. Argus took a spot under the table.

"I ran into Billy Simpson today," Tim said.

"How's he doing, do you think?" I asked. Billy had dumped his wife several months ago for some very solid reasons.

"Actually, he seems to have developed a personality now that she isn't running his life."

"He's finally free of that nut job? Interesting!" I

replied.

"He is in the process of divorcing her and getting on with his life."

"To divorce!" I toasted.

"Amen!" agreed Tim.

The timer went off and the cornbread was ready. I served up the bowls of chili and the plate of cornbread. We ate in comfortable silence and then we had honey molasses cake and decaf coffee by the fire.

Sometime during the night Tim's cell phone rang. Tim talked briefly and then got up and got dressed.

"What's up?" I asked.

"Possible robbery," replied Tim.

"Can't your people handle it until morning?"

"It's Rhonda's store," answered Tim.

It was a chilly morning and at 5:00 am it was still dark. Officer Janet Murphy was surveying the broken front window of Erebus as Tim and I pulled up in his Ford Explorer. Rhonda drove in as we got out of the SUV.

"What the hell?" exclaimed Rhonda as she looked at the broken glass.

"I found it like this when I made my rounds this morning. Do you have an alarm system Ms. Shepherd?" asked Officer Murphy.

"No. I didn't think there would be a black market in stolen Ouija boards and Tarot cards."

"Rhonda, if you would go through the store and

make a list of damages and missing items, Officer Murphy here will write out the report," said Tim.

"Sure, shouldn't take too long," replied Rhonda.

"Let's go get some breakfast," Tim said to me.

"Sounds good. I'll bring something back for you, Rhonda."

"Thanks," she replied as she unlocked the door to Erebus.

Tim and I headed down to Ruby's restaurant on foot.

"Any ideas what that was about?" I asked Tim once we were seated.

"There have been several robberies in Brunswick in the last few weeks. We haven't had any here until now."

"Drug addicts?"

"Most likely. I think if we had an answer to the drug problems, crime in this country would be cut in half."

"And," I added, "There is always greed."

"There is that," replied Tim.

After we finished our breakfast I had the waiter wrap up a breakfast sandwich and ordered a coffee to go. I knew Rhonda would be hungry after the shock of the robbery wore off. Tim set off for the police station, and I let myself into Erebus through the back door.

I set the coffee and sandwich on the counter in the front of the store.

"Thanks. I didn't realize how hungry I was," said Rhonda as she took a bite of the sandwich.

"So what's missing?" I asked.

"The only things missing are a ceremonial knife called an *atheme* and a set of glass beads. They also cracked open the cash drawer, but I only keep a hundred dollars in the drawer overnight."

"Hardly worth their while," I remarked.

"I know. Now I have to have the window replaced and get a new cash drawer."

"Insurance?" I asked.

"Very good coverage, actually. Thanks to my insurance agent."

"Jackson Bennett Associates?"

"Of course," Rhonda replied. "Though I have to offer some special services in exchange."

"I don't even want to know what that means," I said.

I excused myself as soon as I could. I needed to get home and rescue Argus. I don't like to leave him alone in his crate for too long. I wasn't planning to work at Erebus today. This was Tuesday and it was my work-at-home day. I started with doing some house cleaning and then I sat at the kitchen table with my recipe box and started to go through it. I sipped my usual can of Moxie as I worked.

I was looking for some traditional recipes that I could adapt as vegetarian dishes. Since my last physical revealed elevated cholesterol levels, I figured I needed to cut down on saturated fat. If I could collect enough recipes, my book agent assured me we could publish another cookbook. Looking through my recipes cards wasn't helpful. Most of my favorite comfort foods relied heavily on ground beef, pork, or chicken. It was going to take me a lot of background research to get this project going.

I was getting discouraged looking at my recipe cards, when I came upon the shepherd's pie card. Maybe if I substituted lentils and onions for the ground beef, and sweet potatoes for the regular potatoes, it might just work. I jotted down the notes I'd need just as the phone rang.

I glanced at the caller ID and saw that it was Monica. "What's up?" I asked. Monica Ashworth-Twist is my first cousin. She is two years younger than I. We grew up together and were close until she married Jerry Twist and moved to Georgia. Now she was back in Maine and engaged to my old friend Jason Goulet. Jason, Tim, and I had been friends back in high school.

"Wedding plans," replied Monica.

"Have you set a date?" I asked.

"Finally!"

"And?" I prodded.

"The first Saturday in November."

"Congratulations! You're not getting married because you have to, are you?" I asked. At fifty-two, Monica was well beyond the need for birth control.

"Fuck off!" she replied.

"And?" I prodded again. I knew there was more.

"Jason and I would like you to cater the wedding."

"What?" I wasn't prepared for this one.

"It's only going to be a few close friends. Plus his kids and my kids if they decide to come."

"So about how many people are we talking about?" I asked.

"No more than twenty." That was a number I could easily handle.

"Okay," I answered.

"You're a peach," she said and hung up.

It was time to take Argus out for a walk. The dog had an uncanny internal clock. He wanted to take a walk at the same time every day. Except on rainy or cold days and then I have to push him outside long enough to do his business. Since school had resumed, the town seemed deserted. Argus and I walked the nearby streets and didn't see a soul. As we walked by the seemingly empty houses, I wondered how many were unlocked or easily broken into. Rhonda's robbery was making me look at security in a different way. I hadn't locked my house when I left it this morning.

I wouldn't be seeing Tim for a few days. His daughter Jessica was due back from Florida where her mother and stepfather lived. Tim was going to the airport to pick her up; then they were going camping in the White Mountains for a few days. I was invited, but declined. They needed some time together, and besides, the closest I ever get to camping is spending a night in a Motel 6! Enough said!

When Argus and I got back from our walk, I gave Bill Simpson a call. I left him a message on his voice mail inviting him to dinner. I wasn't certain he would accept because I wasn't sure how he was dealing with divorce. But

Stephen E. Stanley

in any case I would be here if he needed to talk.

Chapter 4

The afternoon had turned warm, and summer still lingered in the air. Argus and I sat out on the porch watching the birds taking turns at the bird feeder. I was remembering what it was like to be inside a classroom on those not-so-long-ago Septembers. After a summer of freedom it had been difficult to be stuck inside feeling the warm air filtering in from the open windows. I looked up the street and saw Bill Simpson waving at me. I waved back.

"Thanks for the invite," he said as he came up the steps.

"No problem. I'm trying out a new recipe and I needed a guinea pig."

"I'm always up for a new thrill," he replied.

"Beer?" I asked.

"I won't say no."

Bill took a seat in the living room, and Argus followed me into the kitchen where I grabbed two beers.

"So how have you been, Bill?" I asked as I handed him the beer.

"Not bad. I know that this sounds awful, but I'm really glad to be free and be myself. No more Becky to give me a running commentary on my life."

"No argument from me." The timer rang and I took the shepherd's pie out of the oven. After we sat at the table, we continued our conversation.

"You were in church Sunday," I began. "Did you see

anything unusual?"

"No. I actually was an usher. I handed Jack Riley my collection plate in the back of the church. We put all the money in a velvet sack and put it in one offering plate and Jack took it to the front of the church. After that I lost track of him."

"When did you hear about the murder?"

"Not until later. I left during the organ postlude at the end."

"Were there a lot of new people on Sunday?" I asked.

"There were a few more than usual. This was Homecoming Sunday and most of the people who stayed away during the summer were back. I did see about a dozen people I didn't recognize, but that doesn't really mean much does it?"

"No," I sighed. "It really doesn't mean much."

We spent the rest of the evening sitting on the back screen porch and getting caught up. I hadn't seen much of him during the summer. Bill had gone to stay with his sister in upstate New York during the unpleasantness with his soon-to-be ex wife. He had also spent two weeks sailing on a windjammer out of Camden with my old friend Parker Reed. I ended up driving Billy home because he had finished off close to four or five beers as near as I could tell.

The sunlight was streaming through the open window as I was trying to wake up. Argus was sitting on the edge of the bed waiting for me to take him outside for potty duty and then feed him. After we completed our early morning routine, I was able to sit at the kitchen table with my coffee and paper. I scanned the headlines to see if there were any developments about the murder. A major weather event had moved through one of the western square states and created major damage. The weather catastrophe had knocked the murder out of the headlines.

Jack Riley's obituary was on page nine of the paper. The funeral was going to be on Friday. I called Tim's cell phone and left him a message. I knew he would want to be at the funeral. Today was going to be a busy day.

I whipped up some muffins and put them in the oven while I showered and shaved. I was working at Erebus this morning, coming back home to mow the lawn, and then going out for choir practice in the evening. Once the muffins were out of the oven and cooled off, I packed them up, put Argus in his harness, and we headed off to work.

"Good morning," I said as I entered the store. I passed the bag of muffins to Rhonda. Today she was dressed in a 1970's pink polyester pant suit.

"Blueberry?" she asked as she opened the bag.

"Blackberry muffins, actually."

"Hot shit! I'll go get the coffee," Rhonda replied and headed to the coffee pot.

After our coffee break, Rhonda left to run some errands, and I looked after the store. Business was slow after Labor Day because most of the tourists had gone back to work. I knew business would pick up again when the foliage tours started in October.

Tim called later that morning and said he and his daughter Jessica would cut their camping trip short, and he would be back for the funeral on Friday. I thought about the "fun" of sleeping on the hard ground in a frosty tent, eating dehydrated food, and I breathed a sigh of relief that I hadn't been bitten by the camping bug. Sleeping on the hard ground under a leaky tent with the nearest bathroom about half a mile away just doesn't ring my bells. I prefer a soft mattress, 300 thread count sheets, turn down service, and mints on my pillow.

When Rhonda returned, Argus and I went into the back office and I worked on the Internet orders. Business was picking up, and I thought it was time for me to update the web page and create a more extensive online catalog. Maybe I could get Rhonda to write a daily blog for the website. This project would take me a few weeks to complete, but it would be worth it.

Rhonda sent out for some sandwiches, and I worked until early afternoon and then decided to call it a day. The great thing about working part-time for a friend is that you can call your own shots.

I put Argus in his harness and we started for home. As we passed All Souls Church, I noticed that a cleaning company van had backed up to the rear door. I remembered that there were professional cleaning companies that specialized in cleaning up suicides and crimes scenes. It gave me the creeps that they were now in the choir room cleaning up after Jack Riley's murder.

It was warm in the late afternoon. I had fallen asleep on the sofa with Argus snuggled up against me taking his own afternoon nap. It always takes me a few minutes to orient myself after a nap. Far off I could hear the sounds of a lawn mower. I looked out to see John Lowell mowing his lawn. I hadn't seen either of the Lowells for a day or two and was relieved to know they were okay. They are rather elderly and I try to keep track of them.

The leftovers from last night's shepherd's pie were all I had in the house, so I nuked it in the microwave for dinner. It was choir night and I dreaded going into the newly-cleaned choir room. Argus always knows when it was choir night because my evening routine is different. It must be the way I rush around to get ready, because as soon as I do, he heads for his crate and waits for me to leave.

Though I really don't have much of a singing voice, I do like to sing. So far no one has kicked me out of the choir for the occasional off pitch! I'm also not overly religious, so it might seem out of character for me to be singing in church. But the fact is that I think there is spirituality in humankind that needs to be expressed, and there is a need to belong to a community. There is also a need to stand up for social justice and work to fight poverty and political oppression. And because All Souls Parish Church was part of a liberal denomination, so far no one has thrown me out of church.

The choir room looked the same as always. There was just a hint of chemical smell in the air. We all took out our music and began practicing the anthem for Sunday. Robert Sinclair, the choir director was, at twenty-five, the youngest in the room. There were twelve of us in the choir and we were all over the age of fifty. Robert tried to make the best of what talent he had to work with. Tonight we just weren't getting the music and there was tension in the air. Suddenly Robert stopped rehearsal.

"OK, we really should talk about what happened here in this room and then let it go. We can't do anything to change what has happened, but we can offer Sunday's anthem as a memorial," he said to us.

After we had talked it through for a few minutes, we returned to practicing and rehearsal ran much smoother. It was toward the end of rehearsal that I noticed something wasn't right in the choir room. Sometimes it's what you don't see, rather than what you do see. I probably wouldn't have noticed that something was missing, if a breeze hadn't blown the door to the choir room shut. Normally there was a door stop that keeps the choir room door open, but it was gone!

Officer Janet Murphy was taking down notes as Robert and I tried to describe the missing door stop.

"It was a brick that the church ladies had covered with needlepoint decorations," I said.

"They made a bunch of them last year for the annual crafts' fair, and I bought one for the choir room," added

Robert.

"What did the needlepoint look like?" asked Janet.

"It had musical notes on it and a trumpet or some type of horn it," I said.

"Are there anymore around?" she asked.

"Pastor Mary has one like it in her office," answered Rob.

"Can I see it?" asked Janet.

"Sure, I have a key," answered Robert.

We walked down the hallway toward Mary's office. Robert opened the door with his key, and we found the door stop behind the door. This one was decorated with a lamb and a cross, but otherwise looked like the one from the music room.

"I'm taking this with me," said officer Murphy, "so the coroner can compare it to the head wound." She wrote out a receipt and gave it to Robert to give to the pastor.

Chapter 5

The Pu Pu platter arrived at our table. "And that's about all I know, so far." I was filling Tim in on what had happened in the last few days. Tim, his daughter Jessica, and I were having dinner at Wong Ho's Chinese Restaurant out on route one.

"I wonder where the brick is now?" asked Jessica. Jessica was in her sophomore year at the University of Maine, and she was due to begin classes in less than a week.

"Probably at the bottom of the river," replied Tim.

"Or it could have been thrown into a pile of bricks somewhere. What better hiding place," I added.

"Most likely we will never find it," said Tim.

"If it really was the murder weapon," I said between bites.

"The body has been released. The autopsy results should be on my desk by tomorrow," said Tim. Our main courses arrive and we changed the subject and talked about Jessica's upcoming school year. Jessica was majoring in criminal justice at the university. I was pretty sure that it was a tribute to her father.

"I read somewhere in an article for one of my classes that a murderer sometimes will go to the victim's funeral," said Jessica, referring back to our earlier conversation.

"That's why I'll be there and sitting in the back of the church. I'm going to take note of who is there," said Tim as he finished off the last of General Gao's chicken. "Jesse will be there with me, but I can always use another pair of eyes."

"Thanks dad, but I'll be packing to go back to school. And there are some friends I want to see before I go."

"No problem," answered Tim.

"And," added Jessica, "I don't want to cramp your style." Tim turned red as Jessica winked at me. The kid was cool.

My garden was looking overgrown and seedy as I cut down some stems and withered blossoms. The flowers of summer had passed and it was time to pick the pumpkins and squash that I had grown. I had already canned the beets and carrots. The pumpkin and squash I would have to freeze. That was fine with me as freezing is much easier than canning.

It was early morning and cool, but I had already broken a sweat working in the garden. Argus was sitting in the shade watching me work and looking content. Jack Riley's funeral was at eleven, but I still had time to work in the garden. I dreaded the first frost of the year because it would signal the end of the growing season. Autumn is great, but winter is long and dreary and seems to last just a few months too long.

My thoughts on the season were interrupted by the ringing of my cell phone. It was Tim.

"I just got the coroner's report," he said. "The blunt trauma to the head was the cause of death. And the brick matches the blow to the head almost exactly."

"What about the cloth covering?" I asked.

"That wouldn't cushion the blow enough to make

much of a difference."

"There's more isn't there?" I asked. I could tell by the tone of his voice.

"Yes, there is more. Jack Riley was dying. He had advanced intestinal cancer and had only about a month to live."

"Wow! Someone killed a dying man?" I asked.

"They probably didn't know he was dying. According to the coroner, Jack had a very aggressive type of cancer. He may have felt unwell, but if he hadn't seen a doctor, he might not have known."

"Wow!" was all I could say at this point. Tim told me he would pick me up for the funeral a little after ten. He wanted to get there to observe who came and went.

People were slowly gathering in the church and you could hear the hushed voices from the various seats. I was sitting in the back row with Tim. If Tim Mallory thought he was being inconspicuous in a dark suit, he hadn't looked in the mirror. Tim dressed in a uniform, was striking, but in a dark suit, white shirt and red tie, he looked more like a movie star. Sucks to be him!

As usually happens in churches, people were seating themselves in the back of the church first. The family was down front, then there was a bunch of empty pews and the back was filling up fast. I recognized about half of the people coming in, but the other half were complete strangers. I wasn't sure how much we would find out here, but Tim was furiously taking notes.

"What are you doing?" I asked in a whisper.

"Taking notes!" Tim shot back.

"I can see that much!"

"I'm making lists of mourners. Family, church leaders, school board members, and business associates."

"How can you tell who is who?" I asked. Certain police procedures were beyond my abilities.

"People tend to sit together in groups. What do you see when you look at the left middle pews?" he asked.

"Church groups," I answered as I looked over.

"Exactly! And that group over there," he pointed to another pew, "are the school board members."

"Okay," I answered. I never would have figured that out.

"Mind of I join you assholes?" said a voice from behind. I looked up and saw all six foot seven inches of Jason Goulet.

"Nice talk!" I said and Tim and I slide over to make room for him to sit. Jason, Tim, and I were best buddies back in high school. Actually, Jason and I were in the same second grade at the Huse School.

"Nice box," said Jason as he checked out the casket in the front of the church.

"Waste of good wood," I replied.

"Shut up you two," said Tim.

"What's with Captain Kangaroo?" whispered Jason.

"Working," I whispered back. Tim shot us a look

Stephen E. Stanley

and we both stopped talking.

The music began signaling the start of the service. The family was taken to the front of the church. I guessed the two younger members to be the son and daughter, and two of the older adults to be siblings. Okay, so I was getting the hang of this.

Pastor Mary Bailey began the service, which was named a celebration of life. I had a feeling that more than a few people had shown up to make sure Jack Riley was really dead. I was waiting to see if a band of little people singing "Ding Dong, The Witch is Dead!" would dance down the aisle. I tried to get a look at the notes that Tim was furiously writing down, but the light was bad and his writing was incomprehensible.

After the first hymn Mary made a few statements and then a few of Jack's contemporaries got up and made some remarks. I think the term "damned by faint praise" was appropriate for the remarks I heard.

"He loved to play devil's advocate," said one coworker. Translated that meant he was oppositional defiant.

"Though we didn't always agree with each other," said his son John Junior, "he was still my father."

"Ouch!" whispered Jason when he heard that. I looked around the church. I didn't see anyone who really looked like they were mourning. How unpopular was this guy anyway?

"Quite a list there," I whispered when I looked over at Tim's notes.

"Lots of people are here for such an unpopular guy," Tim replied.

"It might be helpful to figure out who should be here, but isn't," I said.

"Check out the widow," said Jason loud enough for both of us to hear. I looked to the front pew to see Molly Riley convulsing with sobs. She rocked back and forth and her sobbing was getting louder and louder.

"Poor thing," I said until I realized that she wasn't sobbing at all. She was trying to suppress hysterical laughter!

There were finger sandwiches, vegetable dip, cookies, and coffee in the church hall after the funeral. People must be hungry because food was disappearing quickly.

"What was that all about?" I asked. "I missed whatever it was that set the widow off on her laughing jag." There were five of us gathered in one corner of the parish hall.

"Well," began Mark Anderson the high school principal. "One of Jack's co-workers was going on and on about what a great guy he was. When he said that Jack always put others before himself, it was just too much for Molly."

"And everyone else," I added. After Molly Riley began laughing, the laughter was contagious and pockets of nervous laughter broke out all over the church. The speaker was embarrassed at being caught in such a fiction and left the podium. Pastor Mary had to step in with a prayer to keep the funeral from going down the toilet.

"He was on the school board, wasn't he Mark?" asked Tim. "You had to work with him. What was he like?" I could tell that Tim was digging for information.

"I hate to speak ill of the dead," began Mark and then proceeded to tell us what an asshole Jack Riley was.

"Where's Monica?" I asked Jason to change the subject.

"She said she didn't know the man, doesn't like funerals, and wasn't coming under any circumstances!"

"Sounds like her," I responded.

Tim was looking longingly at the finger sandwiches. I thought they looked a little dry and had a little too much mayo in them. I suggested that Jason, Tim, and I pay our respects and go back to Eagle's Nest for a late lunch. We made our way over to the family, offered our sympathy, and then left the parish hall.

The crisp air of autumn and the smell of cooking made for a pleasant atmosphere. Argus had settled himself on the sofa between Tim and Jason, while he watched me with one eye open as I worked in the kitchen. I was heating up the baked beans I had made yesterday and taking biscuits out of the oven. In the microwave I was reheating some macaroni and cheese. All I had to do now was set the table and take out three chilled bottles of beer.

"Food's ready!" I yelled from the kitchen. Argus was

the first one to arrive, followed by Jason and Tim. We all took our places, which meant that the humans sat at the table and Argus sat under it at our feet.

"To good friends," Jason offered as a toast. We clinked our glasses together. "And I wanted to ask you guys something."

"Yes," I asked.

"Monica and I would like you both to stand up with us at the wedding." Jason smiled and seemed to relax.

"We would love to," answered Tim. "Who else is in the bridal party?"

"Just you two. We are going to keep it very small. No tuxedos, no bride's maids, no bull shit."

"And, I'm catering so we'll have to make some plans with Monica," I added.

"This should be fun," said Tim as he took his finger and made a cutting motion at his throat.

After dinner I served port wine and we sat by the fire talking late into the evening.

Chapter 6

A storm was coming. The first indication was the change in the wind. Suddenly the trees were showing the underside of their leaves; then the clouds started to gather on the horizon and advance across the sky like celestial soldiers. Soon it began to sprinkle and the sky grew darker. Finally the heavens opened up and a heavy rain began to fall.

I had planned to putter outside this morning, but the storm would make that impossible. I had managed to get Argus out the door to do his business before the heaviest of the rains hit. I shifted gears and decided to work on my new cookbook. I was planning to call this one *The Bohemian Vegetarian Cookbook*, providing of course, that I could come up with enough good recipes. But I did have a plan. First I would go through my recipe box and look for recipes that contained no meat. Then I would see which ones I could use by substituting tofu or beans for meat. Then I would have to invent some new recipes. I knew I wouldn't get rich, but it was a nice creative hobby. My first cookbook, *White Trash Cooking,* had gotten me all of four hundred dollars in royalties, but it was some extra spending money.

For most of the morning I sat and worked at the kitchen table with Argus at my feet. Tim called me from the road. He was taking his daughter up to the university in Orono for the fall semester.

"If you had just killed someone with a brick, what would you do with it?" he asked me.

"Are you thinking about work?" I asked. I had to

think for a minute. "Well, I probably would take it with me and get rid of it somewhere, or I would have gotten rid of it right away."

"And where would you go to get rid of it immediately?

I tried to picture the area in my head. "I'd walk across the street to the park and throw it into the pond."

"Exactly what I was thinking," said Tim. "I'll call the station and have one of my people check it out."

"I wish I had people," I said.

"You have more people than anyone I know."

"Did you get Jessica, settled into her dorm?" I asked.

"Yes. I always feel a tug at my heart when I have to leave her. But she couldn't wait to get rid of me," Tim sighed.

"Oh, to be young again," I said.

"No thanks," he answered. "Life is great right now. I'll be home for dinner. See you then," and he rang off.

By late afternoon I got tired of sitting at the table working on recipes. It was still raining so I thought I would do some housework. Scrubbing toilets always gives me a sense of accomplishment, but it doesn't take much to make me happy I guess.

Argus and I took a break on the sofa. I must have fallen asleep because the next thing I knew the phone was ringing, and I had to gather my wits about me before I could even find the receiver.

It was the doctor's office reminding me that I had my annual checkup tomorrow. I considered canceling, but didn't. Sitting naked on a cold steel examining table under bright lights while someone pokes and prods me is not my idea of a party.

Argus and I settled back on the sofa and I was just drifting off when the phone rang once again. I was tempted to yank the thing out of the wall. I checked the caller ID, but didn't recognize the number.

"Hello?"

"Hi, Jesse, it's Mark Anderson." Why was the high school principal calling me?

"Hi Mark, what's up?" I asked.

"I called to ask a favor. I have an English teacher who is taking a short leave of absence and I need a substitute teacher. The pickings are kind of slim. I was wondering if you might be interested?"

"You want me to be a substitute teacher?" I asked. I looked behind me to see if any pigs were flying out of my ass. I didn't see any.

"Yes. I already called Amoskeag High School and they gave you excellent references. You would be teaching honors English to high school seniors, just like you did in the past."

"When do you need to know?" I asked. I was conflicted. I liked teaching and it was a good assignment, but substitute pay was dismal.

"The sooner the better. She leaves a week from Monday. And the school board is willing to pay you standard scale *per diem* instead of sub pay."

I had to consider. Thirty years in the classroom with advanced degrees would put me at the top of the pay scale. If it didn't work out, they could always find someone else.

"Sure, I'll do it!" I said

"Thanks, Jesse. I appreciate your help. Come in a little early on Monday and we'll fill out the paperwork."

I hung up the phone wondering what the hell I had let myself in for?

Rhonda was screaming at me on the other end of the phone. "You did what? Are you crazy?"

"It's only for a short time," I said. "They are going to pay me the *per diem* rate."

"Well, it's not like you'll be under contract. If it's awful you can just get through."

"And I'll be teaching Honors English with seniors. I'll do my Erebus work after school." I knew the Internet sales would be on her mind. "Maybe we should look for some part time help for the store. I'll write up an ad for the *Times-Record*."

"That's a great idea. So when do you start?"

"A week from Monday," I answered.

"Have you told Tim yet?"

"No. He's coming over later."

"What about Argus? He's so used to having you home all day now."

"I went over to see John and Dorothy Lowell and

they offered to look after Argus. I'll drop him off in the morning and pick him up after school."

"Well, sounds like you have all the bases covered." Rhonda sighed.

"Don't forget I am a graduate of Morse High. It might be fun to teach in the school where I was a student."

"Well, I'm sure you'll have plenty of stories to tell me!"

"For sure," I answered.

The rain had stopped the next morning, but the air was cold and damp. The examining room was chilly as I sat on the edge of the table in my underwear as Dr. Harry Kahill poked around my abdomen. I knew Harry was a member of All Souls Church.

"Were you in church last Sunday" I asked.

"Yes, but I got called out early for an emergency before the end of the service, so I missed all the excitement," replied Harry as he was hitting my kneecaps with a rubber hammer.

"Did you see anything unusual?" I asked.

"Not really, no. There were more people in church than usual, I thought, but nothing out of the ordinary."

"You are on the board of trustees at the church aren't you?" I asked.

"Yes, I am. So was Jack."

"Did you notice any changes with him in the last few weeks?   Anything seem to be bothering him?"

"Everything bothered him. He questioned and challenged everything new and every idea we had. But that was nothing different," replied Harry.

"It seems," I said as Harry thumped my back listening for something, "that no one liked him."

"He was one of the most unpopular men I've ever known."

"Someone hated him enough to kill him," I said.

"That would be a long list," said Harry as he stuck a tongue depressor down my throat.

It had been a week since Jack Riley kicked the bucket in church. Or I guess someone kicked his bucket for him. I was robed up and sitting in the choir stall with the rest of the singers. Pastor Mary Bailey was halfway through her sermon, then there would be prayers and the collection, and then we would sing the anthem. I had a great view of the congregation from here. Had I been paying attention last week, I might have noticed something unusual. Instead I was studying my music, which I should be doing now.

It was then that I spotted something out of place. From my seat I could see the back of the church where the balcony was located. The balcony was only used during holidays when there was a large crowd. Most Sundays it was roped off. In the center of the balcony was the door to the steeple. I was pretty sure that the door was usually closed. Today it was open. It might mean nothing, but it would be worth checking out after the service.

The anthem was "Onward Through the Ages" and when we were finished the collection was brought down to the front of the church. I was watching carefully to see what was done with the collection. It was placed on the side of the communion table and at the end of the service, a trustee took it away. Last week Jack Riley took it away before the end of the service. It wouldn't have been noticed by most people.

We were all a little hesitant to go back to the choir room and entered as a group, but of course there was no body this time.

Tim was waiting for me outside the choir room when I had disrobed. I told him about the steeple door being open.

"I don't think the officers would have checked the steeple. They were more interested in the crime scene."

"Let's check it out," I said. He headed down the hallway into the church and up the stairs to the balcony.

"Don't touch the doorknob," said Tim as I reached for it. The door was ajar, so I pushed it open. The steeple had a narrow stairway that seemed to reach up forever. A rope hung down from the bell through the floor. One of the ushers would pull on the rope by the front doors every Sunday to ring the bell.

I'm afraid of heights and wasn't sure I wanted to go up the stairs. Tim started up without hesitation. Not wanting to appear to be a whoosie, I followed him, but clung very tightly to the railing.

"Did your detectives find anything when they

searched the pond?" I asked.

"They found plenty of trash, but they didn't find any bricks."

"So much for that theory."

I found a light switch on the wall and flipped it on. The steeple was flooded with light.

"That's much better," said Tim

"I don't know about that. Now I can see all the dust and spider webs." Then I saw the ladder as I looked up. It led to a trap door. "Are you going up there?" I asked.

"Why not?" Tim replied. I could think of about twenty reasons why not, but before I could protest Tim had climbed the ladder and opened the trap door. I followed him up the ladder. We emerged onto an open air platform where the bell was positioned. Above us was more steeple, and I wasn't about to go any higher. I stayed at the top of the ladder. I wasn't about to go onto an open platform at this height.

"Look over there!" I pointed to something in the corner by one of the bell supports. Tim went over to examine it.

"Looks like a rolled up choir robe," said Tim. He went over to it and picked it up. Out rolled a needlepoint covered brick with musical notes on it. It also had a stain on one side of it. Tim picked up his cell phone. "Get a crime kit over here," Tim said to the police dispatcher, and then he turned to me and said "Bingo!"

Chapter 7

The morning air smelled fresh and there was a slight dampness in the air. Tim had gotten up early and gone home to change for work. Argus and I sat on the porch with my morning coffee. The smell of blueberry muffins baking in the oven was making me hungry. I was planning to take them to work at Erebus. Once I started teaching there would be no leisure time in the morning. I would have to get up early and get myself to school. I wasn't sure I was up to it after all.

After the muffins were cool enough to pack, I harnessed up Argus, and we headed out to the shop. It was a good day for walking as it was neither too hot nor too cold. Argus was prancing along like a show dog with his tail tightly curled and his head in the air.

"You are a freaking saint," said Rhonda when I handed her the bag of muffins. She went to the coffee pot and poured out two cups of coffee. Above the coffee pot Rhonda had posted a sign that read "Give Me Some Coffee and Nobody Gets Hurt!" That said it all.

"I'm having a panic attack about going back to teaching," I said after a swallow of coffee.

"Suck it up," replied Rhonda. "It's only for a few weeks."

"I know. But it's so nice to have a leisurely schedule."

"Get over it! You need a little discipline in your life."

"Thanks," I said.

"So what else is new?" asked Rhonda when we were on our second muffin. I told her how Tim and I had gone up into the church steeple. Then I told her about the brick we found wrapped in a choir robe in the corner of the bell tower.

"How did it get up there?" asked Rhonda in amazement.

"Tim's theory is that whoever killed Jack hid the brick in the robe and then went up into the steeple until everyone went home. There is a ladder that goes up beyond the open bell platform up into the upper steeple. No one would think to look there. When the coast was clear he could come down and slip away."

"And," added Rhonda, "he would have a great view in all directions from up there."

"True enough," I agreed. Argus had already settled down in his bed under my desk and was asleep. "I should get to work. I'm going to start by writing the want ad for part time help for the shop."

"We might have some interesting applications in this bad economy," said Rhonda.

"Yes, we might," I agreed as I flipped on the computer screen.

It was late afternoon and Argus and I were ready to head back to Eagle's Nest. I had faxed over the help wanted ad to the *Times Record*. Rhonda's shop was doing quite well, and she wanted to take some time off. She already had me and Brad Watkins, who was now a senior at Morse High. He only came in to work part time, so Rhonda could well afford to hire one more part timer.

"Hey Jesse," said Brad as he came through the door.

"Hi Brad. How's it going?" I asked.

"Not bad. School sucks." As he said that I realized he would know the teacher I would be subbing for and could give me some background.

"Do you know Mrs. Vargas?" I asked.

"Sure, I have her for Honors English class. She's a complete flake. But she knows her material."

"I'm going to sub for her next week," I said.

"You're going to be a teacher? Cool!" And then it dawned on me that Brad had heard me on numerous occasions use the F word, and caught me manhandling the chief of police more than once. It might make for a strange student-teacher relationship. He must have read my mind. "Don't worry. I'll pretend I don't know you."

"Thanks," I said. "That might be best."

"For both of us!" he laughed.

"Okay, Argus and I are heading out. Rhonda is out doing some errands and you are in charge."

The walk back to Eagle's Nest was uneventful, though the town seemed busier this afternoon than it was in the morning. I guess that was natural. John Lowell was out working in his yard as I came up the street. The Lowells, though elderly, had one of the best kept front yards in the neighborhood.

"John, you are putting the rest of us to shame," I

greeted him as we passed by.

"It gives me something to do. Any news about Jack Riley's death that you've heard?"

"Nothing new, really. You saw the article in the morning paper about finding the brick used in the murder. That's about all we know right now," I answered. People always thought that I knew more about what's going on because I was "friends" with the police chief. Actually they were probably right.

Dorothy Lowell came out and invited me in for tea and cookies. I accepted. Why not?

It was one of those September days when the sun shone brightly and the sky was a deep blue. It was around eighty degree and so pleasant that I couldn't envision that winter was coming. Tim had the day off and this would be the last time we would have a weekday together for a while. I would be teaching every day for a week or two and Monday seemed to be approaching fast. We decided to spend the morning at Popham Beach.

We dropped Argus off at the Lowells for a trial run before I went back to school. Tim drove us to the beach, and we parked in front of the fort. Fort Popham was built in 1862 as fortification to protect Maine's capital city of Augusta and the various Bath shipyards from invasion by the Confederates during the Civil War. Construction was halted in 1867 before it was completed. It was a granite fortress and most of the stones had come from a nearby island.

Stephen E. Stanley

No one was around and we wandered around the fort. I had brought my camera and we took photos of each other in various poses along the granite fortification. We took our shoes off and left them in the truck and walked the beach barefoot. Tim was more relaxed than I had ever seen him. Usually his mind is on work even when he's not at the station.

"When are you retiring?" I asked, though I knew what the standard response was going to be

"Another year. I can't wait if retirement is going to be as relaxing as this."

"I know you and you'll need something to do or you'll go crazy."

"I can find something to do. I just want to be in charge of myself and not have to worry about a whole police department."

"It would be nice having you around more often."

"Really?" Tim had a look in his eyes I had never seen before. Suddenly he wasn't the tough cop.

"Yes, Really!" I said. He nodded and touched my hand and we walked on.

We had lunch at Spinney's. The restaurant has been at Popham for as long as I could remember. Eating there always took me back to being a teenager when eating out at Spinney's was a great adventure.

We had avoided talking about work for the most part, but since it was beer and burger time I broached the subject.

"Anything new in the Riley case?" I asked.

"Nothing really. One interesting fact, though. It seems like everyone in his circle knew he had terminal cancer."

"Really? So whoever killed him knew he was dying? That's odd."

"If it was a random act, then the killer really didn't know who Jack was. He might have been after the money and panicked when he heard the church service end.

"Or she," I replied. "Not all killers are men."

"True enough," agreed Tim.

"You think this was a random act?" I asked.

"No, I don't. Jack Riley was unpopular and had too many enemies."

"I'm sure you'll solve the case," I said. "After all you caught the last killer we had."

"Actually, you caught the killer. I just did the arrest."

"Well, maybe I can help this time," I offered.

"You," said Tim pointing at me, "Stay out of it. You take terrible risks."

"Okay, I'll stay out of it," I replied. Like that's going to happen! No need to upset the big guy though.

After lunch we headed back to Bath. It was still a warm and perfect day. We stopped at the Lowells and picked up Argus. He seemed no worse for wear, so I was relieved to know he would be fine when I went back to teaching, however briefly.

With a glass of wine in my hand I headed to the

kitchen and threw some flour and water in the food processor and made pizza dough. I took out some of my canned tomato sauce, fresh vegetables, and cheese and made a pizza. Tim and I made quick work of the pizza. I blamed it on the fresh air and exercise at the beach. Rock and roll!

When I came back from cleaning up in the kitchen, Tim was fast asleep on the sofa. Argus had cuddled up with Tim and he, too, was asleep. Tim was looking very tired. I had seen a side of him today I hadn't noticed before. Something was bothering him. I didn't have the heart to wake him, so I let him sleep and went off to bed.

During the night I had to make a middle-age trip to the bathroom. Tim had come to bed at some point and was hanging off the edge of the bed. Argus had wedged himself between us and was snoring away.

Around dawn Tim's cell phone rang. He jumped out of bed and grabbed the phone. After he hung up I looked at him with sleepy eyes.

"Wazat?" I tried to say.

"There has been another robbery downtown." He got dressed and left.

"The man makes Brad Pitt look like a troll," I said to Argus. Argus had no answer for that so he put his head back down and went to sleep.

It was late morning when I got to Erebus. It was another great day, as it was neither too hot nor too cold. I was glad I wasn't in school during this stretch of warm weather. I selfishly hoped that it would rain next week when I started subbing.

"You are late this morning," was how Rhonda greeted me. Argus headed straight for his bed

"I'm enjoying my freedom while I can," I replied.

"I don't blame you. I'd be a basket case. I've had three replies to my advertisement. They're coming in today and I want you here to help with the interviews.

"Well. This should be fun," I said. "We'll see what the tide brings in."

I was in the back room tweaking the Erebus web page when I heard the bell on the shop door ring and Rhonda bellow out "Jesse!" When I went out to the front of the shop I immediately saw the problem.

"I've come to apply for the position," said a thirty-something woman with shoulder length blonde hair. The problem was the way she was dressed. Rhonda was always flamboyant in the way she dressed, but there was one look she couldn't tolerate and this woman had it in spades. She was wearing a denim jumper with a turtleneck knitted blouse, white ankle socks and Birkenstock sandals. I thought it best to take over the interview at this point since Rhonda was apoplectic with fashion shock.

"As you know, this is a part-time position. Your responsibilities would be sales and inventory. Some evening and weekend work would be expected." I said to the woman. "If you are interested please fill out the application."

The woman dutifully filled out the application and

handed it to me. I looked at her work experience and was impressed with her retail credentials.

"In your work statement you say that you think you would be especially helpful with our line of New Age products. Could you elaborate?" I asked.

"I'm a witch," she said.

"Aren't we all!" replied Rhonda who had once again gained the power of speech.

"No, I mean I'm a Wiccan, a Pagan," she replied. Ronda's eyes were bugging out of her head. This was getting better and better! "I have a working knowledge of what products would be most useful to Pagan community and the New Agers out there."

"Thank you for coming in," I said. "We'll let you know either way."

"Yes, thanks for coming in," echoed Rhonda. The woman exited out through the front door.

"Well, you were a fucking big help!" I said to Rhonda.

"But you saw the way she was dressed!" Rhonda said defensively.

"You are not hiring a model," I replied. "And I'll bet she's the only Pagan you get who applies, though I think one witch is enough for any store."

"Very funny!"

I grabbed the application and headed back to my desk to call her references. The name on the application was Viola Vickner. Interesting name!

Later in the afternoon the wind had changed directions and warm, humid air was coming in from the south. Argus and I prepared to go home. The two other job candidates had failed to appear, so it looked like Viola would be getting the job. Her references had checked out, and I was sure she would be great for the shop. Rhonda wasn't so sure.

"I say we hire her," I said to Rhonda.

"Wait a minute. It's my store and I'm in charge," she replied.

"Sweetie," I said to her, "You are never in charge!"

"Asshole," muttered Rhonda. I called Viola and told her she could start in the morning.

When Argus and I arrived home, Tim was already there and dressed in gray sweats drinking a beer and watching TV. He greeted us and then walked into the kitchen to get me a beer. I was pretty sure he wasn't wearing any underwear.

"What's up?" I asked as he handed me a beer and gave Argus a doggie cookie.

"Nothing much. I left work early. I'm not making any progress on the Riley murder and the town manager is calling me every few hours for an update. I'm too old for this shit!"

"Relax! Let's have a nice dinner and then sit down and go over what we know so far. You haven't told me much about the investigation yet anyway." I went to the kitchen and began to make dinner. I emptied a can of black beans, rinsed them off, mashed them, and added an egg, some seasonings and breadcrumbs. I formed them into burgers and rolled them in more breadcrumbs. I cut up some sweet potato fries to bake in the oven. Suddenly I felt Tim's hands on my shoulders.

"Is it my imagination or are we now vegetarians?" he asked.

"Not entirely. I'm trying a few new recipes out for a new cookbook."

"You are a piece of work!" said Tim with a firm grip on me. I turned around to face him.

"What's up with you? It's not like you to leave work early. And not that I don't love having you around, because I do, but you're spending more time here than usual."

"I don't know," said Tim. "I guess I'm just feeling a little sorry for myself. Jessica is all grown up and doesn't need me anymore. I'm not making much progress on the Riley case, and by the way, Jack Riley was our age. Does it all come down to just a wooden box buried in the ground?"

"It might and it might not," I answered. "I think the important thing here is to live life fully and celebrate what's good and try to counteract what's not as best as we can. You work too hard and you have a tough job. Let's just plan to get away for a few weeks."

"I'd like that," agreed Tim. He hesitated for a moment. "Eagle's Nest is one place where I feel safe." That made me choke up a little.

"By the way," I said pointing to the sweat suit. "I'm

doing a wardrobe inspection later and you better be wearing underwear."

"And if I'm not?" Tim asked smiling.

"You'll see," I answered.

Chapter 8

Rhonda took the bag of muffins out of my hands and set it down on the counter. "Viola starts this morning."

"And that's a good thing," I replied.

"She better not be..." Rhonda started to say as Viola made a grand entrance in to the store. She was wearing a black dress with a long purple cape, a large silver pentagram around her neck, and she had a large walking stick. This was going to be fun!

"Bright blessings everyone!" Viola said as she swept into the room. I thought Rhonda's color had faded somewhat. I was afraid she might faint.

"Good morning!" I said to Viola. "Tolerance," I whispered to Rhonda. I was having a hard time keeping a straight face. "Well, I should get to work." I headed to my desk in the back room where Argus was already asleep on his bed.

By noon Argus and Viola were fast friends. Argus recognized a true lover of nature who had respect for all living things. She offered to look after Argus if I wanted to take a lunch break. I called Tim at work.

"Can you take a lunch break?" I asked.

"I'm the boss," he said. "I can do whatever I want!"

"You must be feeling better."

"Yes, actually I am. Thanks"

"Wong Ho's?"

"Sure, Chinese food sounds good. I'll pick you up at

12:30."

Wong Ho's was a typical Chinese restaurant, with lots of red paint, smiling dragons, and paper lanterns. We took a seat in a booth.

"Mind if I talk shop?" Tim asked.

"Not at all. You just have to agree to listen to me talk shop when I go back to teaching."

"It's a deal. I need you to keep your ears open for any church gossip. You might hear something from your involvement in church."

"I'm in the choir and on the community committee. Neither of which Jack Riley belonged to." I replied.

"True, but check for any members in those groups who might have been on a committee with Jack."

"You think someone at church might have killed him." I asked.

"Probably not, but he was killed *at* church."

"True enough!" I answered. We placed our order with the waitress.

"I think it more likely that someone who had a professional grudge against him did it."

"What exactly did he do? I know he worked for a small company, but that's all I know." I said.

"He co-owned a computer software company called Island Software, Incorporated. They create software for city and town government agencies."

"Co-owned? I asked. "What about the other owner?"

"Her name is Kathy Bowen. She has an alibi for the Sunday he was killed. We're checking out the other workers now."

"And don't forget the school board. It could be any angry parent or teacher for that matter." I added.

"I know. It seems impossible!" Just then out food arrived and we changed the subject.

When I got home later the message light on my answer phone was flashing. I pressed the button and listened.

"This is Dr. Kahill's office. Dr. Kahill would like to see you first thing tomorrow morning." It was too late to call the doctor's office back. Leaving a message like that for anyone over the age of forty was a sure guarantee of a sleepless night.

At nine o'clock the next day I was sitting in the examination room waiting for the doctor. I was reading his diplomas and certificates on the wall just to pass the time.

"Good morning Jesse," he said when he came into the room.

"What's wrong?" I asked. I was getting nervous.

"Nothing really. Your cholesterol is still high. I want to put you on a cholesterol lowering prescription." I began to relax.

"That's all?" I was relieved.

"Left untreated it could be serious. I'll send the prescription in."

"Okay. I couldn't help but notice your certificate

from the South American Physician Volunteers. You must know my friend Alex Tate. He was one of the founders." Alex was my college roommate at Southern Maine University. He was a biology major and I was an English major. He helped me out in science and I helped him write papers. He went on to medical school and was one of the few African Americans to open up a medical practice in New Hampshire.

"Sure," he hesitated. "I met him once in Ecuador."

In a few minutes I was out the door and on my way home. I was almost sure that Alex Tate hadn't worked in Ecuador, but I suppose it's easy to get mixed up. I glanced at my watch and said aloud, "There's ninety minutes of my life I won't get back."

Time was slipping away. Only a few days left before I started teaching again. I told myself it was no big deal. It was, after all, only for a week or two, but still I wasn't sure I could do it. It was also choir practice night, which meant there were only two weekdays, then the weekend, and then back to school. I had to stop obsessing about it.

We gathered in the choir room for practice around seven-thirty. As true to form several people were late. Rob Sinclair looked at the clock and decided to start with some stretching exercises and then some vocal warm-ups. By eight o'clock only half the usual number had shown up.

"Where is everyone?" asked Rob.

"I think people were really uncomfortable here after

the murder and decided to stay home," replied Julie Morris, the lead soprano.

"Well, I need to scrap the piece I had planned and choose something easier for a smaller choir. Let's get out of here and rehearse in the church," said Rob. I wasn't sure there would be any good music for an eight member choir, but what the heck.

"Maybe more will show up on Sunday morning," I said hopefully.

"I hope you're right," replied Rob. We rehearsed "Morning Has Broken" and it didn't sound all that bad.

A cold air front was coming in from Canada, and I knew it was time to celebrate the coming of fall. Each year I made a crab and corn chowder and Rhonda and I would get together for a fall celebration. Last year we had included our new friends, and I intended to make it an annual tradition.

It was Friday morning and I was working at Erebus. It was my last "free" day for a while, since I would be starting school. I was making my shopping list and calling people to invite them over for Saturday. In between phone calls, I filled orders for Erebus.

Viola seemed to be working out okay, and Rhonda was happy. At the moment I was alone in the store. I could hear the bell if anyone came into the front. I left messages for everyone I called. It seems no one answers their phones anymore. I heard the bell and went into the front of the store.

"All by yourself?" asked Tim.

"Yes, I'm actually closing up today." I hadn't seen Tim in two days. He had been working extra shifts.

"I need some personal activity time," said Tim and he locked the shop door and put a "Be Right Back" sign in the window.

"Would these be age-appropriate activities?" I asked.

"Of course not!" answered Tim.

"Good to know," I said and waved Tim into the back room.

Chapter 9

Jason and Monica were the first to arrive at Eagle's Nest. It was good timing because we had wedding plans to talk over.

"If I'm going to cater this wedding," I said as I opened the door to let them in, "I need to have a number and know what you want for food."

"Chill, Jesse. It's very informal and we've got a month to plan," said Monica.

"We've already talked with Mary Bailey and have the church hall reserved," added Jason as I showed them into the living room.

"Buffet finger food would be fine. We are not hosting the Windsors you know," Monica rolled her eyes at me.

"Okay, I'll work out a menu for you to look at," I said just as Tim walked through the door.

"Hey Mallory," greeted Jason, "What's new in cop land?"

"What's new is that I just sent in my retirement letter to the city manager," Tim replied as he looked at me. There was a stunned silence.

"Good for you! I thought you were waiting one more year," I replied.

"Life is too short. Anyway it's not happening until June. Then my pension will kick in," said Tim as he picked up an excited Argus off the floor.

"We'll need a big celebration," said Monica.

Rhonda and her flame Jackson Bennett arrived and

Argus rushed to greet them. Argus loved a house full of company.

"Hi everyone! What's new?" asked Jackson. Tim told them his news. Rhonda screamed and ran to Tim to give him a hug.

"You'll love retirement!" said Rhonda. "No one can fire you!"

"That's true," I said. "I need to put the biscuits in the oven. Tim, would you be the bartender? There are chilled glasses in the freezer." The kitchen was nice and warm, thanks to my French cook stove. I set the kitchen table for six as I had no dining room. I stuck the biscuits in the oven, set the timer, and returned to the living room. Tim had made me a cosmopolitan.

"Maybe you could be a bartender," I said as I sipped my cosmo. It really was very good.

"I just want to work for fun," said Tim. "I don't want to be in charge anymore."

"Jesse will be thrilled to have you around!" said Rhonda.

"I don't know about that," I said. "He's pretty high maintenance."

"High maintenance? How so?" asked Rhonda. I just rolled my eyes.

"Oh, that!" she said just as the timer went off.

"Supper is ready!" I said in my best Maine dialect.

We sat down and I ladled out the corn and crab chowder and passed around the cornmeal biscuits.

"To life!" said Jackson as a toast. We all lifted up our glasses.

"To life!" we all repeated.

Everyone was quiet as they tasted the food. I always hold my breath until the first compliments arrive. Argus had sprawled out under the table with his chin on my foot.

"This is great!"

"Yummy!"

"You outdid yourself."

"Thanks guys," I said. It's always nice to hear compliments. I remember someone saying that if you can cook, you'll never be without friends. Jason and Monica talked about their upcoming wedding; Jackson and Rhonda talked about taking a trip to Montreal; Tim talked about retirement; and I talked about going back to school. When we finished eating we adjourned to the living room for a glass of port.

"How's the Riley investigation going?" asked Jackson.

"Nothing new," answered Tim. "Except that today I learned that Riley often went out of town for days at a time and no one at his business knows why."

"Did you ask his wife?" I wanted to know.

"Not yet" answered Tim. "I'm saving up several questions for her later."

"Never mind about dead people," interjected Monica, "What's for dessert?"

"Sour cream chocolate cake," I said.

"And why" asked Rhonda, "Isn't a slice sitting in front of me right now?"

"Why indeed?" I answered and went to slice the cake.

By the time everyone left I was too tired to clean up. I took Argus outside for his nightly duty and crawled into bed. During the night I had vivid dreams of being late for school, being unable to find the right room, and walking into a classroom of midgets. Substitute teaching was becoming way too stressful, and I had as yet not even gone into the school. I drifted in and out of sleep until the smell of freshly brewed coffee woke me up. Tim had come in on his way to work and had loaded up the dishwasher, cleaned my kitchen, and made coffee.

"I thought you might need some help this morning and I was right," said Tim as he handed me a cup of coffee.

"Thanks, I was too tired to clean up last night. And look at you, all this work and not one crease in your uniform or a hair out of place."

"Will this buy me some points?" Tim asked.

"Big time!" I answered. "I guess you won't be going to church if you're all dressed up for work."

"There was another break-in last night. It was the coffee shop,"

"First Erebus and then the coffee shop? The robbers can't be too bright. There's not much money in either place."

"I don't think it's about the money," said Tim. "I think it's about something else."

"Like what?" I asked.

"I'm not sure. Get dressed and I'll take you to Ruby's for breakfast. Maybe we can figure something out."

We sat in front of the window at Ruby's and had a nice view of the river. The restaurant was crowded even for a Sunday morning, but when the chief of police shows up in uniform, a table suddenly becomes available. Our orders were served promptly.

"So do you think that the break-ins here are related to the break-ins over in Brunswick?" I asked.

"No, I don't. I talked to the chief in Brunswick. We compared notes and there are some real differences in the two sets of forced entries. I think that the Bath robberies are copycat crimes. On the surface they seem to be similar, but there are some significant differences."

"Like what?" I asked.

"For one thing the Brunswick crimes netted significantly more money, and they used more sophisticated entry means. They were able to disable alarms and jimmy the locks. The Bath crimes were crude. They smashed windows to get in and the coffee shop had an alarm system which they weren't able to disarm."

"But no clues?"

"None," said Tim.

I looked at my watch. "Show time," I said and

headed out the door for church.

Jack Riley's murder had been good for church attendance. For the last two Sundays there had been a significant increase in visitors. I'd like to think that the attention to mortality had made people more introspected, but most likely they were just curious. Several more choir members showed up for the morning rehearsal, so we were almost a full choir again.

Church began with the opening hymn and the choir processed down the aisle. As I looked at the robed figures ahead of me I suddenly had a thought. What better disguise in a church than a choir robe? The killer could have worn a robe and been hanging around outside the choir room. Nobody would think that strange at all. The robe closet was unlocked and there were plenty of unused robes there. I'd have to mention it to Tim later.

As I was sitting there I took a quick inventory of who was and who was not in church. I knew Tim was working, Jason and Monica were sitting in the back and so were Rhonda and Jackson. I hadn't seen Billy Simpson in church for the last two weeks. I'd have to check on him later. It was time for the anthem and we stood and sang "Morning Has Broken." We did a fine job if I say so myself, and there was spontaneous applause when we finished.

After church I hurried home to savor my last afternoon of freedom before I started school in the morning. I gathered up Argus and we drove to Popham Beach. Each year, before school started in September, I would go for a walk on the beach. Going in to substitute for two weeks or so wasn't exactly the same, but I saw no reason to break with tradition. I hadn't been in the classroom for over a year, and I needed the beach!

Argus loved the beach. There was nobody else around, and I was able to let him off his leash. As I walked along the beach Argus ran around me in happy circles. Every once in a while he would creep down to the water's edge until a wave came in and then he would jump back before the wave would hit. The sound of the waves, the cry of the gulls, and the smell of the sea always have a calming effect. I'm always reminded of poet Matthew Arnold's words : "Listen! you hear the grating roar / Of pebbles which the waves suck back, and fling, /At their return, up the high strand, / Begin, and cease, and then again begin…"

I broke into a run and Argus ran after me. After a few minutes we were both out of breath. "Time to go home Argus," I said. I snapped the leash on him and we headed back to the car. I was feeling overwhelmed. I had my new cookbook to work on, a wedding to plan, my days filled up with teaching, an Internet business to work on, not to mention just the day to day stuff that needs to get done.

"I'll be glad when this substitute stint is done," I said to Argus. He just looked at me with one eye and drifted off to sleep.

Chapter 10

I was awake well before the alarm went off Monday morning. I haven't used an alarm clock in over twenty years, but I wanted to make sure I was on time. It was another example of my deteriorating mental condition since I agreed to sub.

The original building of Morse High School had changed very little over the years. Various wings had been added over time, each representative of the decade in which it had been built. The original building was built in 1929, replacing an earlier one that had burned to the ground. I remembered all those mornings back in the seventies when a group of us would sit on the granite front steps and wait for school to begin.

"Rock and roll," I said to myself as I headed into the building and found the main office. Mark Anderson had the papers ready for me to sign, gave me directions to my room, and wished me good luck.

My room was on the second floor of the old building. I remembered it because it had been my homeroom during my senior year. There was a bust of Shakespeare mounted above the chalkboard in the front of the room. I sat down and looked at the lesson plans that had been left for me. I was in luck! I was to teach Chaucer's *Canterbury Tales*. I knew it well and it would last for at least the time I was subbing.

The bell rang and students filed into the room. I took attendance from the seating chart, introduced myself, and launched into my lecture on the Medieval period. If they thought they were getting a substitute who was going to give them a study period, they had the wrong guy. After a short introduction to Chaucer, I had them open their books to Chaucer's "Prologue."

"I'm going to read the opening to 'The Prologue' and I want you to follow along in your books." I stood in the front of the room, closed my book, and then recited the Prologue from memory. They were duly impressed. Of course after you teach the same thing for thirty years, you pick up a few skills.

I assigned homework, the bell rang, and the students left the room. I now had four minutes before I had to do the whole thing over again, and then do it over again two more times after that.

After school, I picked up Argus at the Lowells. He seemed to be none the worse for a day away from home.

"Did you notice the 'for sale' sign across the street?" Dorothy Lowell asked.

"No, I didn't," I answered. I had no idea who lived there. There were only four houses on the street and we all knew each other, except for these people. They had a two car garage with automatic door openers. I would see cars approach and then disappear into the garage. As far as I know they never went outside. They even had a lawn service come, so they wouldn't have to go outside.

"Well, good riddance I say," said John. "Unfriendly

sons-of-bitches."

"Let's hope we don't have a family with ten kids buy the place," I said.

"Let's hope," said Dorothy.

I took Argus home and collapsed on the sofa. It had been a fun day, but I was exhausted. Brad Watkins was in my last class of the day. He nodded to me, took his seat, and pretended not to know me. I'd see him at Erebus after school tomorrow. I knew better than to plan on going into Erebus on a Monday.

Tim called later and said he would take me out for dinner tomorrow night. I had some leftovers for tonight, and I'd spend the rest of the evening preparing for tomorrow's lessons.

The second day of classes went well. I gave a pop quiz on the "Prologue" and we continued with Chaucer's description of the pilgrims. These were good students and they seemed to have a grasp on character development. Everything ran like clockwork until the third period when we all had to empty the building for a fire drill. Fire drills, principal announcements over the intercom, and unscheduled assemblies are the scourge of the teachers' world. Fortunately I only had to deal with one of those today.

The worse part of the day was cafeteria duty. Almost every teacher gets stuck on this duty sometime during his or her career. A few unlucky souls get stuck with it year after year. I circulated around the cafeteria watching and listening. There was a lot to be learned about students from careful observation. One of the things teachers look for as they circulate among the students is any sign of abuse. Many times in my career I've taken note of black and blue bruises and, more often than not, they were inflected by a parent or relative, and I've had to report suspected abuse to the authorities. So much for family values!

There was one group of boys sitting at a table in the corner that I was keeping my eye on. I knew the ring leader from my last period class. There was something going on that I couldn't put my finger on. I stood near the group and pretended to look in another direction, but listened to snippets of their conversation. I decided to ask Brad Watkins to fill me in on the group later.

I called the Lowells at the end of school just to make sure that they were okay looking after Argus. Everything was fine and I set off down the hill to Erebus. The weather was cool and dry; it was a perfect autumn day. The leaves were beginning to turn and they would be very colorful in about a week.

Viola was working when I got to the shop. She was wearing a bright red Gypsy skirt and a matching red hat. Rhonda was nowhere in sight.

"Hi Viola, How's the job working out?" I asked.

"Hi Jesse, I love it. I get to talk to people when they come in, and I get plenty of time off as well."

"I know. I love working part time," I said. "Brad should be here soon and then you can go home."

"I'm sure my cats miss me. Where's Argus?" she

asked.

"My neighbors are dog sitting while I'm subbing."

"Hey Jesse! Hey Viola!" Greeted Brad as he walked through the door.

"Hey yourself!" I said to Brad. "I haven't seen you in about thirty-five minutes."

"Okay," said Viola. "I'm out of here!" She waved and swept out of the shop.

"She's something else!" remarked Brad.

"I wish I could be here when Rhonda and Viola are both here. Kaboom!" I said and made a hand gesture for emphasis.

"Me, too," replied Brad.

"I'm going in the office and work on Internet orders. Are you all set here?" I asked.

"Sure. It shouldn't be too busy."

I started up the computer, checked email, and then processed some orders. I packed up orders for shipping just in time for the UPS pickup. It was close to closing time. Tim would be stopping by to take me to dinner soon.

"Hey, Brad, what's the story with Peter Thompson and his band of merry men?" I asked, referring to the group of teens I noticed while on cafeteria duty.

"Peter Thompson is an asshole!" said Brad. "He and his posse are bad news."

"How so?" I asked.

"They are serious druggies. They deal at school, but they've never been caught. And you never heard it from me."

"Hear what?" I asked innocently. "By the way how am I doing at school?"

"Actually the kids like you better than Mrs. Vargas. You're not as tightly wound as she is. She makes us all nervous."

"Hey guys, what's up?" asked Tim as he stepped into the shop. He was wearing tan Dockers and a fisherman knit sweater.

"Hi Mr. Mallory," replied Brad. "You must be off duty."

"I don't always wear the uniform, only when I have to be in public. This was an office workday. Are you ready for dinner?" Tim asked.

"Are you okay to close up?" I asked Brad.

"Sure thing, Mr. Ashworth!" answered Brad.

"Where to?" I asked Tim once we were outside.

"How about Maxwell's? It's just down the street and the food is good."

"As long as they have beer," I said.

The hostess sat us in the window. I could look up the street and see the Bath Savings Bank and down the street and see the fading painted sign for Povich's Men's Shop on the side of a brick building. There were a few people still walking along the sidewalks. Maxwell's had exposed brick walls and ornate tin ceilings and was very cozy. We both ordered draft beer.

"How was your teaching day?" asked Tim.

"Much easier than I thought it would be. I taught Chaucer for thirty years, and kids are pretty much the same anywhere. It was kind of fun, but takes much more energy than I remember."

"You want to do it full time?" he asked.

"God, no! I have too much to do. I need to work on my new cookbook, plan Monica's and Jason's wedding, work around the house, and take naps! How was your day?" I asked.

"My day was bullshit!" said Tim. "I spent the day on paperwork and personnel issues. I much prefer being out and doing real work. The thing I like least about being in charge is all the paper work."

"You know anything about drug dealers in the school?" I asked.

"Nothing official. I know there might be a problem, but no one is talking to the police. And I'm sure Mark Anderson doesn't want any bad publicity with the school board he's saddled with."

"Give me a day or two and I might have a lead."

"Good, I'll put some of my officers on it." We ordered our dinner. I had broiled scallops and Tim ordered baked haddock.

"How's Jessica?" I asked.

"My daughter must be having a great time. She's not coming home until Thanksgiving."

"Well, she's with people her own age who share her interests. It must be dull here."

"Must be," answered Tim. "I'm off tomorrow. You mind if I hang out at your place for the day. I can take care of Argus and get dinner for you."

"Tim, you have a key and you know my place is yours!"

"Of course. I just need to hear it now and then."

"Are you okay?" I asked.

"Just feeling disoriented, I guess. I really want to retire on one hand, and I really don't on the other."

"I know exactly what you are going through. It's the end of something you've spent your whole life doing, and there is nothing yet to take its place. It will be great, but you have to work through it yourself."

We finished dinner, picked up Argus from the Lowells, and headed back to Eagle's Nest. I sat and corrected the day's quizzes while Tim watched TV with Argus. Before we turned in I made a to-do list for the week, just so I wouldn't forget anything.

The morning was clear and cold. Off in the distance I heard the honking of geese as they gathered together for their winter migration. Tim was up before me and made coffee and toast. All I had to do was get out of bed, shower, and get dressed. I could get used to this.

It was Wednesday and I had three more days of school to get through. I had more than enough material, I just wasn't sure I had the energy. It was strange being in the high school. I had spent my high school years there, so many things were familiar and comforting. There were memories around every corner. On the other hand, I was a teacher and it felt strange to be at the school.

"Are you going to choir practice tonight?" Tim asked as I was packing up to leave for school.

"Probably, unless I'm exhausted, which is a real possibility," I answered.

By ten o'clock in the morning I was dragging, and I was pretty sure I wouldn't be going to choir practice. There was a special, unannounced assembly that pretty much ruined my lessons for the day. No wonder the Vargas woman was taking time off! During lunch duty I kept my eye on the little Peter Thompson group. There was something wrong there, I was sure. I saw money change hands several times, and I was quite sure that they were not exchanging lunch money. There were five of them all together, and three of them I recognized from class; the other two I didn't know.

When I took attendance during the last class of the day, I noticed that Peter Thompson was absent. Since I had seen him at lunch I knew he had cut my class. I filled out the appropriate paperwork and dropped it off at the end of the day.

Tim was on the phone when I walked through the door. Argus came running up to greet me. He waved at me as he listened with the phone against his ear. I could tell by the way he was speaking that it was a work related call. I looked around the room. There were fresh flowers on the coffee table, a fire in the woodstove, and soup on the stove in the kitchen.

"What's up?" I asked when he got off the phone.

"Nothing much. Just the office calling. There was a house break in this afternoon."

"What's all this?" I asked and wave my hand around the room.

"You're not the only domestic one around. I know how to drive a vacuum cleaner."

"You're very un-cop like," I replied. "But I love it." No way was I going to choir practice tonight!

"Let's have dinner on the back porch," offered Tim.

"It's a little cool for that isn't it?"

"Wait until you see," replied Tim. We went through the kitchen to the back porch. Tim had replaced the screens with glass storm windows. It was warm and bright and he had set a small table with two place settings and candles.

"Wow, this is nice! Where did you get the windows?" I asked.

"I found them stored in the rafters of your garage and thought they might fit. Apparently that's what they were for."

"I saw them, but I thought they were storm windows for the old house windows I had replaced. I almost threw them out." The sun had warmed the porch through the glass and it was very comfortable. I would be able to use it at least for three seasons now. "Do I smell bread?"

"I found your bread machine and used your Anadama bread recipe. And I made split pea soup. And if you look in the 'fridge there is a cosmopolitan waiting."

"You need to take a day off more often!"

"After June, I'll have all my days off," answered Tim.

"I know you and you'll need something to do," I said. I took the drinks out of the refrigerator; we sat and I told him about my day teaching. We had dinner on the warm back porch and watched the day fade into night.

*

Chapter 11

The seasons change in very small, but noticeable increments. In only a matter of days the leaves had changed from green to endless shades of yellows and reds. The first hard frost had arrived and the ground was covered with frost. I had left my car out of the garage and had to find a scrapper and use it on the windshield. The air was crisp and the weather clear. Soon the sun would warm up the day and there would be a thirty degree difference in temperature between morning and afternoon. I took a deep breath of the clear morning air. It was good to be alive!

My week of subbing was drawing to a close. I had enjoyed teaching, but it reminded me of all the hard work that teachers have to do each day. I was looking forward to getting my life back to a more leisurely pace and not having to dress up for work. Tim wasn't used to seeing me dress up in what he called "teacher drag." I wore tan or gray slacks, a colored shirt, and a matching tie. I had lots of ties left over from thirty years of teaching. I wouldn't miss wearing the ties at all. Today and tomorrow I would be wrapping up my unit on *Canterbury Tales*. Today we would be reading "The Pardoner's Tale" and discussing the not-so-veiled references to the corruption of the medieval church.

As usual, the worst part of the day was cafeteria duty. For some reason the students were more hyped up than usual. I'm sure the ninety-minute pep rally had a lot to do with it. I was walking around behind Peter Thompson's table when I caught sight of a metallic flash.

"I'll take that," I said and took the object out of his hands before he could hide it.

"Hey, give that back to me! It's mine! You can't take it!" he yelled.

"I'm pretty sure weapons are a no-no in school," I replied. "And as you may have noticed, I've already taken it."

"Fuck you, asshole! I'll get my father in here!"

I leaned over him and whispered so no one else could hear, "Fuck you and your father!" He looked stunned for a moment. I waited thirty years to say that to a punk. It felt good! What can they do, fire me? "You can ask Mr. Anderson for it later."

I placed the knife on Mark Anderson's desk. He turned it over in his hands. "Nice weapon," he said.

"I liberated it from Peter Thompson," I replied. Mark sighed. "It's not a weapon exactly; it's a ceremonial knife, known as an *atheme*. It's also stolen property from the Erebus shop.

"You're sure?"

"Oh, yes. It's one of a kind hand-engraved with Celtic runes. I know because I'm the one who ordered it for the store."

"Okay, I'll call the police and have them pick up Peter."

"It's been real," I said and headed back to the

classroom for the last class of the day."

After school I headed out to Erebus to tell Rhonda about the knife. It was after three when I got there and Rhonda and Viola were having tea. Rhonda was wearing a 1950's pillbox hat and pearls, and Viola was wearing purple tights and a long red sweater, and she sported a silver pentagram on a chain around her neck.

"I'm sorry," I said. "I didn't know this was a costume party!"

"Well, you're dressed for it too," replied Rhonda. I realized I was still wearing a tie and a baseball cap.

I told her about Peter Thompson and the knife and that most likely the police would be stopping by to ask her to identify it. Just then a box of Q-tips entered the shop. That's what we call a bus load of senior citizens with white hair. Most likely younger people thought Rhonda and I were Q-tips, too, except for the fact that we both still had our natural hair color. Or at least I still did; I wasn't so sure about Rhonda's hair. After the elderly left the store with their purchases, Tim arrived with Officer Janet Murphy. Viola had never seen Tim before.

"My, you're a big guy aren't you?" gushed Viola at Tim.

"She doesn't know the half of it," I whispered to Rhonda, who promptly bit her tongue to keep from laughing.

"Viola, this is Police Chief Mallory and Officer Murphy," I said. Tim produced the knife and Rhonda identified it. I also officially identified it as the stolen property and gave a statement of how I found it.

"Thanks for your cooperation," said Tim as he was leaving. He paused at the door, "I'll see you tonight, Jesse?"

"Sure, I'll pick up something for our breakfast tomorrow," I answered. I watched the smile freeze on Viola's lips.

"Nice meeting you, Viola," said Tim and breezed out the door.

I went to my desk in the back room and left Rhonda to fill in any blanks for Viola. More orders than I'd ever seen before were waiting to be filled. It finally occurred to me that people were shopping for their Halloween festivities. At five I left the shop, went to the grocery store, and stopped at the Lowells to pick up Argus. Argus was glad to see me, and I was sure he missed his daily routine. I started to make a vegetable pie for dinner. I wasn't sure what time Tim was coming, so I got it ready to pop in the oven when he got here.

Sometime later Argus heard Tim's truck before I did and ran to wait by the door. Tim had already changed into his civvies and had a six pack of Seadog in his hand.

"If that woman flirts with me again, I might have to shoot her," said Tim as he passed me a bottle of ale.

"Don't shoot her," I replied. "She's providing me with an entertainment element. I love to see Rhonda and Viola try to outdo each other." I popped the pie in the oven.

"What was with the outfits?" he asked.

"Rhonda has always been slightly flamboyant.

You've seen her Fourth of July outfits, and her Christmas costumes, but when Viola came in dressed as the wicked witch of the west, all bets were off."

"Good work on busting Peter Thompson. He admitted that he did the downtown robberies. He even seemed proud of it. Interesting side bar to the story; he's Jack Riley's nephew!"

"Jack Riley's nephew? Small world."

"Not so surprising in a small town like this," said Tim.

"At least he won't be in school tomorrow. My last day of subbing! I get my life back next week."

"Are you going to do it again?" Tim asked.

"It was fun, but I like my own schedule. I'm done with bells."

"But I like the tie," said Tim as he got up close to me and started to finger my tie. "I like the school teacher look. I've always had a fantasy about English teachers."

"You really are high maintenance," I said. "In a good way, that is."

Friday was warm and dry and it was a perfect fall day. I finished up my sub job by giving a Chaucer unit test. I would leave the corrected tests for Mrs. Vargas to grade as she saw fit. Lunch duty was better today because the Peter Thompson group had been suspended or expelled. The only bad part of the day was looking at the great weather outside and being stuck inside. It was fun being at Morse High again. Around every corner was a memory. I remembered how I used to dress for gym, go to the gym for attendance, and then go back to the locker room, get dressed, and go to the store around the corner for a snack. Good times! At the end of the day, I signed out and was done. Working again for a full week was more tiring than I remembered, but then again, I'm also older. Teaching is a young person's profession.

Tim was working on the weekend, so I was pretty much on my own. I needed to get some housework and laundry done, and I needed to spend some time with Argus. Argus hates the vacuum cleaner so I had to shut him on the back porch while I cleaned the house. When I finished the housework I went into the kitchen to make some coffee for my midmorning break. I measured the water and placed the paper filter in the coffee maker. When I went to open the coffee can, it was empty! I needed coffee now!

Argus was sleeping in a chair on the porch and was safe and sound, so I decided to go the coffee shop for instant gratification and then stop off at the store for coffee beans. Brian Stillwater was standing at the counter pouring steaming milk into a mug of coffee.

"Hey, Brian, what's up?" Brian owned the coffee shop and was known to be a bit eccentric. He was a follower of Native American spirituality and favored Indian dress and jewelry. His dress stood in contrast to his white hair and blue eyes.

"Not much. The police think they found the kids

who broke into my shop."

"Yes, Peter Thompson and his posse."

"My son had you for a teacher this week. He said he liked you." Brian was a single father.

"Thanks for the feedback. It was fun, but I don't think I'll be doing it again."

"Too bad! You couldn't pay me enough to do it ever," he said.

"I've heard that a lot," I replied.

"What can I get you?"

"Give me a tall coffee, breakfast blend cream, no sugar."

"You got it," said Brian as he passed me a cup. I looked around the coffee shop for a place to sit and spotted the widow Riley sitting by herself near the window. Since I knew her slightly from church, I made my way across the room.

"Hi Molly," I said by way of greeting. She had cut her hair since I had seen her last at the funeral. She was dressed in jeans and a sweat shirt, and wasn't wearing any makeup.

"Hi, Jesse," she waved her hand to indicate that I should sit with her.

"I'm so sorry about Jack," I said. "It was an awful shock for all of us."

"Thank you, Jesse. You were one of the first to," she hesitated for a moment and then continued, "to find him."

"Yes, I was. Do you have any idea who might have

killed him? I mean just a suspicion that you might not want to share with the police," I asked.

"I know people didn't like him," she said. "But he was always good to me and the kids."

"What about his business associates?"

"Well, It's only a feeling, but... no maybe I shouldn't say anything," Molly started to say.

"Sometimes feelings lead us in the right direction," I offered.

"I know she has an alibi, but I wouldn't be surprised if Kathy Bowen wasn't behind Jack's murder."

"Kathy Bowen?" I asked. I pretended I had never heard the name.

"She co-owned the business with Jack. They had a huge blowup a few days before he died."

"Really?" I asked. Sometimes it's better to listen than to talk.

"She lost a half million dollar account for the company. Jack wanted to buy her out. She didn't want to be bought out. They had words."

"Did you tell this to the police?" I asked.

"No. I don't have any proof, and I knew she had been out of town on a trip when he was killed."

"Who told you she was on a trip?" I asked Molly.

"Jack did a few days before he died. He was furious that she took the company credit card and left for Washington to lobby for a government contract.

"I thought Island Software created programs for

town governments?" I asked.

"They were trying to get into state and federal agencies."

"I heard Jack often went on business trips," I said.

"Actually, he hardly ever went on business trips. Most of the trips he took were charity work for nonprofit agencies."

"He did what?" I couldn't picture Jack Riley doing charity work. That bird just didn't fly.

"He never let anyone know. People think he was just a jerk. But he gave tons of money and time to charity."

"Did he ever talk to you about the charities?"

"No. He liked to keep that private; I respected that."

Just then one of Molly's friends came over, and I thought it was time to leave. I said my goodbyes and headed toward the door with my coffee.

"Hey, Jesse!" called Brian as I was leaving. "I'm starting a group of open-minded people to discuss spirituality. You interested?"

"I don't know," I answered. "Sane, normal people often turn into nut jobs when you mix in religion."

"Not religion, but spirituality. I know your family used to be free thinkers, and I think you'll be a good fit."

"Sure," I said. What the hell.

"Okay, we're going to meet at my house next week. I'll let you know the day and time. And if you know of others who would be good, bring them along."

"I sure will do that!" I said. I had at least two people

Murder in the Choir Room

I could think of who might just make Brian Stillwater want to take a long hit on the peace pipe.

Chapter 12

A weather front from the south had moved into coastal Maine and the air was hot and humid. People had forgotten about autumn and lived like summer was eternal. Folks flocked to the beaches on their day off and dressed in their summer clothes, which they had yet to put away. My rose bushes by the back porch were blooming and their perfume filled the back yard. After a restful weekend I was ready to face the world again.

Tim had stopped by for dinner on Sunday night, and I had filled him in on my conversation with Molly Riley. Her conviction that Kathy Bowen killed her husband, while interesting, didn't give the police any new leads. Tim was checking into the charity business trips, but they were unlikely to pan out.

I invited Monica over for lunch to talk about the wedding plans. Jason and Tim were working so it would just be the two of us family members. I sat at the kitchen table and made a list of possible food items for the reception. Argus had found a cool corner of the kitchen to curl up in for his morning nap. While I was working on the menus I also took some notes for my new cookbook. It was great to be working on my own stuff again. I was done with school! Been there, done that!

About midmorning I put together a macaroni salad and fruit compote for lunch, and then I went back to planning for the wedding. By the time Monica arrived I had a list put together and prices for each item.

Murder in the Choir Room

"Anyone home" yelled Monica through the front door. Argus ran barking to greet her and led her back to the kitchen.

"Well, aren't you special" I said, "to have a canine escort."

"The dog and I are good!"

"So let's get down to business," I said as I poured her a cup of coffee.

"Here's the budget for the food." She passed me a piece of paper with a monetary figure on it that would be more than enough.

"And how many people will be coming?" I asked.

"I'm inviting twenty, but plan for about twenty-five."

"So here is what I came up with for a menu. I have others on the list that I can add, if needed.

"Lobster salad, Caesar salad, Swedish meatballs, roasted potatoes, steamed vegetables, French bread, Madeleines, and wedding cake," she read off the list. "That should be fine for a light wedding supper."

"It's easy enough to do. I can do most of it ahead and have it ready in the church hall for the reception," I said.

"Wonderful," replied Monica.

"Just one tiny, teeny problem," I added as she looked at me.

"I'm not sure I like the sound of that," she said cautiously.

"I can make a wedding cake, not a problem, but cake

decorating is something that I can't do. You might be better getting a professional to do it."

"No!" she said sharply. "I want a real cake. Not some fake vanilla white cake with plastic frosting. I don't care if it looks like a three year old decorated it. I want your chocolate sour cream cake!"

"You're not going to be one of those crazy brides they show on reality TV are you?"

"We'll see! Oh, and one other little thing you can do for us."

"What would that be?" I asked cautiously.

"Jason and I have decided to dress a little more formally. I'm going to wear a formal, non-wedding dress. We would like you and Tim to wear tuxes since it's an evening wedding."

"We're not going to look like we're going to the prom are we?"

"No, we've picked out something tasteful. You and Tim just have to go get measured. Jason's already been measured."

"You could just elope," I offered.

"And you could go…"

"Ah, ah, language," I interrupted.

"Let's eat," I said to change the subject. We took our lunch plates and our beers out to the back porch and sat in the comfortable rockers and ate. The sun was streaming into the backyard. The birds were flocking to the bird feeder, probably loading up on energy before the long trek south.

Murder in the Choir Room

"I've got a bad feeling about Jack Riley's murder," said Monica out of nowhere.

"Well, it doesn't get any worse than murder," I said.

"No I mean, I don't think this is over. I think you should stay out of it."

"I thought you weren't all that convinced in grandmother's psychic voodoo."

"It wasn't voodoo, and you know as well as I do that we both have a touch of it, and that it's helped us out in the past."

"Okay, but I'm only going to admit this to you, I've got the same bad feeling about this."

"And," Monica added, "I'm worried about Tim." I had a sinking feeling because it confirmed the vague dread I had about this whole thing.

"Me too," I admitted.

"Don't worry," she patted my hand. "We'll figure something out."

Before she left I told her about Brian Stillwater's spiritual discussion group.

"Count me in!" she said.

Unlike many Maine towns, Bath has a long history of diversity. As a shipbuilding town, it has attracted workers from all different backgrounds and welcomed them into the fabric of the community. There had been a few bumps in the road, such as when a group called the "Know Nothings" burned the Catholic Church in the 1840's. But, in most cases

Stephen E. Stanley

Bath has welcomed all.

In the 1880's a large family traveling by rail was forced to stop in Bath because one of the children became sick and needed medical attention. They were so impressed with the kindness of the locals that they decided to remain in Bath and make it their home, becoming one of the first Jewish families to settle in the area.

In the early 1900's a small group of Eastern European refugees found opportunity and safety they could not imagine in the homelands where pogroms were becoming all too frequent. By the late 1920's they had built a synagogue for worship with the help of both Jewish and non-Jewish citizens.

When the house next door sold and I met my new next door neighbor, it was no great surprise that she was wearing a *kippot*, or skull cap, and that she happened to be a rabbi. Argus and I were taking our afternoon walk when we saw her unloading a car in the driveway of the house. She was a short, blonde woman somewhere in her thirties.

"Hello, I'm Jesse Ashworth. I live in the yellow house over there," I said pointing to Eagle's Nest.

"Hello, Jesse. I'm Beth White and I'm just moving in, as you can see." She put out her hand. "And who is this?" she asked as she looked down at Argus. The dog adores women and went wild.

"This is Argus," I said. "Welcome to the neighborhood."

"Thanks, I'm a little overwhelmed with the move, as

you can see."

"What brings you here?" I asked.

"I'm teaching a religious history class at Bowdoin College and helping out as needed at the temple."

"I'm a retired English teacher and I write cookbooks," I replied. "I'll let you get back to unpacking you stuff. If you need anything, feel free to come on over."

"Thanks Jesse, it was nice to meet you."

Hurricane Krystal was due to hit the Florida coast by morning. The news was filled with images of people boarding up their homes and loading up their cars to evacuate the area. There were also those individuals who were shopping for supplies for their hurricane parties. The weather here was warm and sunny, but we knew that in a few days we would be facing a tropical storm, the remnants of the hurricane.

The cranberry scones were cooling on the rack, and I was looking forward to working a full day again at Erebus. I hadn't spent a day at the store yet when both Viola and Rhonda were working. I thought it might be entertaining.

The scones were packed away, and I harnessed Argus up and we headed out. We walked down Sagamore Street onto Crestview to High Street and we passed by Morse High. School was in session and I was glad not to be inside on a nice day like this. We walked down the hill past All Souls Church, through the park, and up Front Street to Erebus.

I passed the bag of scones to Rhonda, unharnessed Argus, and made for the coffee pot.

"Cranberry," I said as a greeting.

"Smells great!" she answered as she looked into the bag. "What's new with you?" I told her about meeting my new neighbor. She told me about her date with Jackson, and then I went into the back office and started up the computer. I checked my email before starting work. After trashing the usual offers for products to enhance manhood and to buy fake degrees, I was left with two real messages. The first was a reminder from the church secretary that Sunday we would have a guest preacher from South America. The other message was from my parents who had just entered the computer age with their first email account. They were retired in Florida and had never shown an interest in coming back. Such a cliché!

By eleven o'clock I had most of the mail orders filled. Viola came into the shop for her afternoon shift. She was wearing what could only be called an over the top gypsy outfit. Rhonda rolled her eyes when Viola came in.

"I think it's good for business," I said.

"I think it might be good for target practice," replied Rhonda.

"Bright blessings everyone," greeted Viola as she swept into the store.

"Are you telling fortunes today?" asked Rhonda in a slightly sarcastic manner.

"What a great idea! I could set up a little table in the

corner and read Tarot cards on the side."

"I was just kidding. I didn't mean…"

"I think it's a great idea!" I interrupted. "I'll help you set up." Rhonda was visibly flustered. I love to stir things up!

By noon Viola and I had cordoned off a corner of the shop with hanging beads and set up a small table for two for her readings. Rhonda was fuming, but she calmed down once she realized this might bring in more business.

"What's my cut?" asked Rhonda.

"How about fifty percent?" replied Viola.

"Here, I think a nice candle on the table will add atmosphere. And maybe a nice paisley table cloth." Suddenly Rhonda was being very helpful.

On the way home I took a detour and decided to go by Bill Simpson's house. Argus always likes it when I vary our walks. Lots of new smells, I guess. I hadn't seen Bill for a week or two and thought I should check on him. Billy had a lot of changes in his life in the last year, and they weren't good ones, for the most part.

As I got closer to the house I could see that something was terribly wrong. The lawn hadn't been cut for some time, the mailbox was overflowing, and newspapers were piling up by the door. I ran up and pounded on the door. I got no answer. I tried the door knob and the door was unlocked. "Come on, Argus," I said as we stepped inside.

I looked around the living room. There had been

Stephen E. Stanley

some significant changes since I was last there. The 1970's decor had been updated, but the room was a mess.

"Hello! Billy? Are you here?" I didn't like the look of this. In the kitchen, it looked like he had been in the middle of preparing breakfast when he was interrupted. A box of corn flakes and an empty bowl were on the table. A half full cup of instant coffee was on the counter by the sink.

Argus began sniffing around and went running into the bedroom. I was afraid if I looked in I'd see a body draped over the bed. There was no body, but the bed was unmade. I checked the other bedroom, the bathroom, and then the basement. No Billy anywhere! I took out my cell phone and called the police.

Chapter 13

Tropical storm Krystal swept in on the first day of October. The warm, moist, strong winds and the driving rain stripped many of the trees of their colorful leaves. If the storm lasted too long there would be very little autumn color this year. The streets were almost empty and people struggled against the wind and rain as they sought shelter inside. Erebus had a busy morning as the foliage tour busses pulled into town.

Viola's Tarot card readings were doing quite well. The added benefit for Rhonda, besides the fifty percent cut, was bringing business to the shop. At my urging, Rhonda had set up a display of New Age books.

I had to force Argus out into the rain to do his business. We took the car to work as I really wasn't up to walking in a tropical storm, or any other storm for that matter. I hadn't baked any goodies this morning because of last night's choir rehearsal, and slept later than usual. I stopped at the coffee shop and picked up some Danish pastry.

Argus greeted Rhonda and then headed to his bed under my desk. I worked for most of the morning and was finished by noon. Jason stopped by to take me to lunch. Viola had arrived at noon, and she promised to look after Argus while I was gone.

"Hey," said Jason when he poked his head around into the back office.

"Hey, yourself," I replied.

"Where do you want to go?"

"How about Maxwell's," I suggested. "It's just down the street and that way we don't have to get too wet." I grabbed my jacket and we darted down the street under the various shops' awnings. The hostess seated us at a table in the window.

"How's Tim?" asked Jason.

"Tim's been working extra this last week, trying to tie up loose ends so he can use up some of his vacation time before retirement." The waitress came with our drinks and we ordered our lunch.

"Any progress on the Riley murder?"

"None, yet. You know how these things are. Somebody will sooner or later trip up and give themselves away. Did you hear about Billy Simpson?" I asked.

"No, what about him?"

"He's missing!" I said.

"What do you mean, he's missing?" I told him about going by the house and finding it empty.

"How long has he been missing?" Jason asked.

"If we use the date of the newspapers as an indication, it's been more than two weeks."

"What did Tim do?"

"There's not much he can do. Adults have the right to disappear if they want. There was no evidence of violence, just a hasty departure. He contacted Billy's daughter, but she hasn't heard from him for over a month. Tim's making some informal inquiries, but officially he can't do much."

"This is all very strange," said Jason.

"I even called Parker Reed, because they were seeing each other, but Parker hasn't heard from him in weeks. He said Bill hasn't returned his calls."

"I feel bad," said Jason. "Billy's been gone for weeks and none of us noticed."

"I know," I replied."What else in life should we be doing if not taking care of each other?" Our food arrived and we were quiet as we ate. The storm had intensified outside, and we lingered over coffee before heading out into the driving rain.

"Are you sure this is the suit they picked out? I look like I belong on the cover of the *Sergeant Pepper*'s album?" I complained as I was being fitted for the wedding.

"It's the style this season," replied the clerk with the measuring tape.

"And the others are wearing the same thing?"

"Mr. Mallory and Mr. Goulet have already been in and fitted."

"Super," I said flatly. However, when I looked in the mirror I was surprised at how flattering the tuxedo was.

"Well, as long as it's what they want," I said to the clerk. It never hurts to dress up once in a while.

After the fitting I went to the store to gather up supplies for the kitchen. I dropped off the supplies at home, picked up Argus, and we took a ride out into the country to check out the farm stands.

The storm had finally passed, and the leaves that were still left on the trees were bright shades of yellow, red, and orange. Argus had his nose out the crack of the window, sniffing all the new smells. It was nice to get out and enjoy the day. Tim was coming over later and we were going to see if we could figure out what was going on with the Riley case.

The farm stands had a rich array of fruits and vegetables. I bought some apples for an apple pie and applesauce to can. I picked out pumpkins and Indian corn for autumn decorations. Squash, turnip, onions, and potatoes would keep for weeks in the cool basement. On the ride home Argus settled into the seat and slept. The day was cool and it was the perfect time for cooking.

When we got home I preheated the oven while I sliced up some apples for the pie and sprinkled them with lemon juice to keep them from turning brown. I mixed and rolled out a whole wheat crust, added white and brown sugar to the apples, mixed in a quarter cup of tapioca to soak up the juices, and put the pie together and placed it in the oven. When it came out of the oven I made a glaze of water and apricot jelly and brushed it on the crust to give it some shine and color. It smelled so good it was all I could do to keep from eating it.

Next, I took a butternut squash, cut it in two, and spooned out the seeds. I made my meatloaf mix using soy protein instead of ground beef, added in minced onion and mild red peppers, and the secret ingredient of a half cup of cola. Then I stuffed the squash with the fake meatloaf mix and put it aside for baking. I next washed and cut up some fresh green beans, and took out my rice cooker and a package of brown rice. When Tim showed up all I would have to do is turn on the rice cooker, put the green beans in the steamer basket over the rice, and throw the squash into the oven.

I still had two hours before Tim was due, so I made a cup of herb tea and took my book to the back porch. The sun was streaming in through the glass windows and the porch was warm. I sat in the rocking chair and Argus jumped into my lap. A dog, a cup of tea, and a book! It doesn't get any better than that!

I must have fallen asleep, because the next thing I knew Argus had jumped down and was barking and Tim was standing in the door.

"Must be nice," said Tim. "Asleep with a dog in your lap in the late afternoon!"

"You should try it sometime," I replied. "It would do you more good than working so many hours"

"I just want to wrap up all the cases on my desk so I can go out with a blaze of glory."

"I'll go start dinner and then we can sit down and review the Riley case." I put the rice in the rice cooker, put the green beans in the steam basket over the rice, and stuck the stuffed squash in the oven. Next I took two bottles of Seadog Ale and passed one to Tim. "Here are some recipe cards. We can jot down notes about the murder on them and see if they make any type of pattern. It worked on the last murder case."

"Sounds like a plan," said Tim as he took a swallow of the ale.

"Okay," I started. "Jack Riley took the collection plate out of the service early. He was not scheduled to be the one to do it."

"And," added Tim. "He was hit on the head and killed in the choir room, where he had no business being." I was furiously scribbling all this down on note cards.

"The murder weapon was a decorated brick that was used as a door stop, which we found later in the steeple wrapped in a choir robe. The killer must have hidden in the steeple after the service," I said.

"Wait!" exclaimed Tim. "Maybe he didn't hide in the steeple. Maybe he planted it later to throw us off!" I was still writing on the note cards trying to catch up.

"And that," I said putting my pen down and looking at Tim, "is why you are the Police Chief!"

"Let's eat!" I said as I got up to serve dinner.

"I see you are cooking with meat again," said Tim as he dug into his food.

"Actually, no," I replied. "It's vegetable protein. No meat anywhere in there."

"You're kidding right? This is awesome."

"Apple pie for dessert, but only after we finish the note cards."

"You're a hard-hearted bastard!" said Tim smiling.

Murder in the Choir Room

We finished eating and I loaded the dish washer.

"Jack Riley was terminally ill," I said as I wrote on a note card. "So why kill a dying man?"

"Good point!" replied Tim.

"And who benefits?" I asked.

"The wife, of course, and Jack's business partner," answered Tim.

"And who hated him?"

"Almost everyone he knew!"

"And what were those mysterious business trips he took that no one seems to know anything about?" I asked.

"Okay," Tim summarized, "We have two questions we need to answer. Why kill a dying man and where did he go on those business trips?" Tim collected the note cards and stacked them on the table. "Time for dessert."

"I'll get the pie out," I said.

"I wasn't talking about the pie," said Tim.

Chapter 14

Another hard frost hit Maine the next morning. The ground was white with frost, and the vegetation was wilted. Once again I had left my car outside the garage, and had to go out and scrape the windshield. The colored leaves had begun to fade and were falling off the trees. I'd have to rake up the leaves pretty soon and get the gardens ready for winter. Make no mistake, winter was coming, and it was coming sooner than later. The days were beginning to be noticeably shorter, and I could feel myself beginning to miss the sunlight.

Tim had left for work, and I planning to spend the day at home, working on the vegetarian cookbook. So far I had collected enough recipes to make a good start, but I still had to field test a few. Most were vegetarian adaptations from my recipe box, and so far had turned out okay. I had just settled down when the doorbell rang.

The doorbell always startles me because it is used so infrequently. Most of my friends just knock on the door, walk in, and yell. Argus hates the doorbell and went tearing off on a run barking as he went. I opened the door and saw Beth White standing on porch.

"I hope I'm not interrupting you," said Beth.

"Not at all, come in! Would you like some coffee?" I asked.

"That would be lovely," she answered. "I'm afraid my kitchen isn't well stocked yet." I ushered her into the living room and went into the kitchen to make a pot of coffee. I took some muffins out of the freezer and zapped them in the microwave. I put everything on a tray and returned to the living room. Argus jumped onto Beth's lap.

"I'm sorry about Argus," I said. "He's not well-behaved and he likes company."

"I love dogs!" said Beth. "If I had more time, I would have one."

"How are you settling in?"

"My oil tank is almost empty. I was hoping you could recommend a good oil company. These muffins are very good, by the way," she said as she tasted a blueberry yogurt muffin."

"Thanks," I said. "I use Benson's Oil, for the furnace, not the muffins. They have a budget plan and automatic fill up, so I never have to think about it. Running out of oil on a cold winter night can be very inconvenient."

"Just what I need. I'll give them a call."

"When do you start teaching at the college?" I asked.

"I've already started with research and writing, but I don't begin teaching until January."

"That's good. It will give you some time to settle in."

"Have you always lived here?" she asked.

"No, I did grow up here, but left after high school. I worked in New Hampshire for thirty years, then I moved back in retirement."

"That must have been an easy move," she replied.

"Actually, no." I then went on to tell her about renovating Eagle's Nest and about finding a buried corpse in the backyard.

"Well, that makes my relocation problems seem insignificant. My problem is that it's hard to meet people in town. Everyone seems to know everyone else."

"It probably seems that way, and I know people's perception is that New Englanders seem cold, but give it a little time and effort and you'll feel at home in no time," I said.

"I hope you're right!"

"Here's an idea. Brian Stillwater, the guy who owns the coffee shop, is starting a spiritual discussion group. Why don't you come along?" I asked.

"I'm not sure," she hesitated.

"It's spiritual, not theological. No fundamentalists!"

"Sure, why not?"

"Okay, I'll let you know when the next one is." I offered.

"I should get going. Thanks, Jesse."

"No problem. See you later."

Choir practice was back to normal. Everyone showed up for rehearsal. The music for Sunday was easy enough that we actually sounded good. It probably was a good thing because most of us were still upset by the sight of a dead man in the choir room. The fact that the murder remained unsolved didn't help our nerves any.

Murder in the Choir Room

"Be here at nine o'clock Sunday morning to rehearse. Remember that we are having a guest preacher, so we need to be a little flexible about time," Rob Sinclair reminded us. We put our music folders away and filed out the door as quickly as possible. No one was inclined to linger behind and chat.

When I was outside I saw a police cruiser parked across the street with its lights off. I went over and slipped into the passenger seat.

"I brought you some decaf and a donut," said Tim from the shadows of the driver's seat.

"What's up?" I asked.

"I'm on the late shift tonight and wanted a break."

"I could use a sugar high myself," I said.

"I'm having second thoughts about retirement."

"I kind of figured that out," I replied.

"In spite of not always working with the cream of society and having to do lots of paperwork, it does have some excitement to it."

"You could be a private cop," I said. "Work for yourself, be your own boss. You'll have your pension to live on. You can just take on the cases you want, when you want." I could sense Tim relaxing in his seat.

" A private detective? I never really thought of that. That's a great idea!"

"Glad to be of service," I said. Tim reached over and ran his fingers through my hair. "You're not going to get all gushy are you?"

"I might," said Tim.

"Awesome," I replied and took another sip of coffee.

Sometime during the night it started to rain and rain hard. I woke up early and left Tim sleeping. Argus followed me into the living room. I had several things to do and going to work at Erebus was low on the list. I took my laptop into the kitchen and started surfing the web for information on cake decorating. I really wanted to practice decorating a cake so the wedding cake for Jason and Monica's wedding would look presentable. I had a vision of a lopsided cake with smeared white and yellow frosting.

By the time Tim woke up I had two layers of cake cooling on a wire rack in the kitchen.

"What the hell are you doing?" asked Tim as he poured his morning coffee.

"And good morning to you, too," I said handing him a plate of scrambled eggs and toast.

"Sorry, you know how it is before coffee in the morning."

"I'm practicing cake decorating before I make a complete fool of myself at the wedding reception. Frosting a cake is something I never mastered. As you may have noticed, I dribble icing or powdered sugar on all my cakes."

"Good luck with that! Did you suggest that they get the cake from a bakery?"

"Yes, and have you ever tried to suggest anything to Monica after she makes up her mind?"

"I see your point," replied Tim

"And what are you doing today? I asked.

"I have to do staff evaluations. It should be a fun day!"

"I sense verbal irony," I answered.

"You sense correctly." Tim finished his breakfast, gave me a hug, and headed off to work. Argus followed Tim to the door and then ran back to the kitchen and curled up under the table.

I got out my recently purchased decorating tools and started to work. I sprayed the cake with a sugar and water mixture and let it dry to help reduce crumbs. Then I spread on a base of white frosting on the cake. I took an icing bag and added yellow edging to the cake. So far it was going to be passable if not perfect. The basic cake was looking good, I'd practice making frosting flowers in the next few days. Since it was about two weeks before the wedding I had a little wiggle time. I'd make the finished cake next week and put it in the freezer. I can't stand to wait to the last minute to do anything.

It was now midmorning and I figured I should make an appearance at Erebus and work on some Internet orders. I cut up the wedding cake to take in with me, otherwise I would be stuck eating wedding cake for the next two weeks. I wrapped up the cake, harnessed up Argus and we headed out the door. I took the car to work because it was raining.

Driving to work was a challenge, as the rain was much heavier than I thought. There were limbs down everywhere and the remaining leaves on the trees had all fallen, leaving the trees bare. Fallen branches and wet leaves made for a difficult drive, even though it was only a little over a mile.

"Bright Blessings!" said Viola by way of greeting when Argus and I walked in the door.

"Good morning," I replied. "Where's the old hag?"

"Jackson took her out to breakfast, and they haven't returned yet."

"Is everything quiet here?" I asked.

"So far it is. I had a few window shoppers, but that was it."

"Okay, I'll be in the back if you need me." Argus headed to his bed under my desk and I pulled up the internet sales. There were more rush orders today than usual, then I realized that Halloween was in less than two weeks. Most of the orders were for occult paraphernalia. By mid afternoon I had the orders ready and waiting for UPS pick up.

Just as I was packing to leave, Rhonda came into the back office with a piece of cake in her hand.

"Good cake," said Rhonda between mouthfuls.

"Thanks, it was practice for the wedding cake."

"Hell, I'd even get married again just for the cake," joked Rhonda.

"You think Jackson's going to pop the question?"

"I don't know. I hope not."

"Why not?" I asked. "He's a nice guy and he adores you."

"I know. It's just that I like things the way they are. Change leads to change."

"I know. I feel the same way. I really hate change. Usually change is never for the good."

"You know," began Rhonda, "we never have any time together any more. We are either working or going about our separate business."

"That's because when we were teaching at Amoskeag High, we were pretty isolated. Here in Bath we've had more time to be out in the real world and meet real people. All we ever saw for thirty years were teenagers and other teachers, most of whom had a very tenuous grasp on reality. It was a very narrow view of life."

"I guess you're right. In this case change was for the better."

"Come on over for supper tonight," I said. "We can talk some more."

"I'll be there!" she answered.

The ride back to Eagle's Nest was just as troublesome as the morning ride had been. The roads were still littered with fallen branches, and the leaves were still wet and slippery. It had stopped raining, which was a good thing. I half expected the lights to be out when I got home, but everything seemed to be in order. The house was extremely cold and damp, so I built a fire in the living room.

Since Rhonda was coming for dinner, I decided to take a break from the vegetarian fare and make a *stifado*, or

Greek beef stew. It's not so much that I'm against meat, but I have a real problem with factory farming and animal mistreatment. For the stew I used farm-raised organic beef. I knew Rhonda liked Greek food, and I had picked up recipe tips from the two summers I spent in Greece back in the eighties. The stew is basically beef and onions with a tomato sauce, currents and spices. It simmers on the stove for about three hours and fills the house with its spicy smell. It is the perfect meal on a cold, damp day. I cut up the beef and onions, added the spices, and put them all on to simmer. I took out the bread machine and tossed in the makings for a nice whole wheat bread.

Once everything was cooking, I got out my cookbook project and started working. Argus was under the table snoozing way. The house was warming up, and then I noticed that it was getting dark out even though it was only late afternoon. I love the change of seasons, but hate the loss of daylight. I went around the house and turned on as many lights as I could to keep the darkness at bay. Argus started barking and headed to the door so I knew Rhonda had arrived. Who needs a door bell when you have a pug?

"This is shitty weather," said Rhonda as she came through the door and handed me a bottle of chardonnay.

"It's nice and warm here, have a seat and I'll uncork the wine." I returned with two chilled wine glasses.

"So what's new with you and the hunky cop?"

"Tim is determined to solve the Riley case before retirement," I answered.

"What's wrong with that?"

"I'm not sure it's solvable. He's also having trouble adjusting to the idea of retirement. I don't think he's in the right frame of mind to let go."

"Well," began Rhonda, "we both know what that's like. It is loss and grief over the end of all you've known, and excitement about all that is now possible. The trick is to relax and go with the flow."

"I did suggest that he become a private cop and work cases he chooses," I offered.

"That's a great idea, just make sure he has some down time before starting something new.".

"And what's new with Jackson" I asked.

"He certainly has no interest in retiring. In fact he is busier than ever. But he still makes time for me. I'm afraid he might ask me to marry him, and half afraid he won't."

"So you said this morning," I reminded her.

"Well, I love things the way they are. We each have our own lives, yet we spend lots of time together and have fun. What we share is quality time. If we got married that could all change. We'd have plenty of time together, but what would happen to quality. Remember, I've been married several times."

"Four times if I'm correct!"

"Fuck you, the first two didn't count."

"Whatever! And why are you afraid he won't ask you?"

"If he doesn't want to marry me, does that mean he

doesn't love me?"

"You are," I said slowly, "overanalyzing the situation. Happiness is not the future; all we have is the present, especially in middle age. We've buried enough friends to know that."

"You are right! *Carpe Diem!* Live for today. And if I might say, dinner smells wonderful."

"It's almost ready. I better go check on it," I said and headed to the kitchen.

The bread was cooling on a rack and I set up a card table in the living room so we could eat by the fire. I refilled the wine glasses and dished out the *stifado* into two bowls. There was plenty left over. I put on some soft Greek background music.

"This is just like a *taverna* in Greece!"

"Without the twelve-hour flight," I added. Argus had sprawled out in front of the fire and was watching us out of the corner of his eye, just in case we were clumsy enough to drop something.

"Enough about me," said Rhonda as she put down here spoon. "What's up with you?"

"I don't know what happened to retirement," I said. "I'm busier now than ever. Jason and Monica's wedding, my new cookbook, helping Tim with the Riley murder."

"But those are all fun things, except for the murder, that is. And even with that you get to work with the hot cop."

"He actually seems to need my support these days. It feels good to be needed," I said.

"I know, I think that's why we're all here," replied Rhonda.

We spent the rest of the evening eating and talking until past midnight.

Chapter 15

Billy Simpson had been missing now for close to a month. My calls to his adult children revealed nothing new. They didn't know where he was, and they hadn't heard from him. They seemed alarmed at the news, but unable to do much about it.

I was getting frustrated with the lack of progress. Tim had done as much as he could officially and had reached a dead end. I decided to launch out on my own. I put Argus in his crate and headed out the door to Billy's house. It was a work day and none of his neighbors seemed to be at home. I went up the steps and rang the front doorbell. I managed to stand in such a position that I blocked the view of his mailbox. There was a pile of new mail in the box. I reached in and scooped out the mail and placed the contents in the bag I had brought along. I was quite positive that this was breaking the law. Oh, well!

I took the bag home and dumped the contents on my kitchen table. I was pretty sure Tim wouldn't approve of my action, but he was very unlikely to find out. Most of the mail consisted of utility bills and junk mail, however there were bank statements and three credit card statements mixed in.

I set the tea kettle on the stove to boil. I had seen TV shows where the characters steam open envelops, but I had no idea if it really worked in real life. Once the water was boiling I held the envelopes up to the steam. I was able to steam them open, but the paper was all soggy. They never showed that part on TV!

Murder in the Choir Room

The American Express card showed no action for the last week of the month. That was worrisome in itself. Of course he might have had another card he was using. The next card also showed no action in the last several weeks. Now I was getting worried. It was clear from looking at the statements that he was in the habit of using them on a weekly basis.

When I opened the bank statement I saw that Bill had taken a large sum of money out of his account just before he disappeared. Now I was stuck with the information. How could I let Tim know, without revealing the fact that I took the mail in the first place? I took the bundle and walked back to Billy's house and left it on the porch. I picked up my cell phone and called Tim.

"Hi. I'm at Billy's house checking on things. He has so much mail that some of it fell out of the box and was lying on the porch floor."

"And?" said Tim in a noncommittal voice.

"Well, two of them seemed to be opened, and I just happened to see what they were."

"You mean you opened them?" asked Tim.

"Of course not," I said, "that would be wrong."

"Of course," replied Tim with a sigh. "As long as they were open and visible, is there something I should know?"

I told him about the credit cards and the bank statements.

"As long as you're there, would you mind giving me

all the account numbers?"

    "Sure," I read them off to him.

    "And if I recall correctly, aren't you a distant relative of Bill Simpson?"

    "Ah, yes sure," I was catching on. I'm sure somewhere in the last three hundred years Billy's family and mine crossed paths.

    "And are you officially filing a missing person report so I can look into it?"

    "Sure," I replied.

    "And if you ever do something like this again, I will throw you in the clink!"

    "Hard ass!" I replied and hung up.

    It was World Peace Sunday and a guest pastor from South America was to be the worship leader for the day. The choir was in church early to rehearse for the service. The Reverend James Foster was a Maine native who had spent the last twenty years working with doctors in the Andes Mountains. The loose collection was going to go to South American Physician Volunteers. There were visitors from other churches and from Maine's denominational office attending today's service. The choir and congregation were invited to an early morning breakfast at the church. For once I didn't have any hand in the church's food preparation as it was catered by a company from Portland.

Murder in the Choir Room

After choir rehearsal I headed down for breakfast. Tim, Jason and Monica, Rhonda and Jackson were sitting with Harry Kahill. They had saved me a seat.

"I hope the music isn't going to suck this morning," said Jason as I sat down.

"You're tone deaf," I replied, "How would you even know?"

"Don't listen to him," said Monica. "I could hear you rehearse, and you all sounded great. The big guy here is just a little cranky."

"Has anyone met the guest of honor yet?" asked Tim.

"I talked to him briefly," said Harry. "He's an interesting guy."

"I hope so. I don't like to be bored in church," cut in Rhonda. "You know how some of these guest preachers are."

"Any information about Billy Simpson?" asked Jason. I just froze in my seat wondering how Tim was going to handle the question.

"Nothing yet. We have a few leads we are following," answered Tim. It sounded exactly like a noncommittal police statement to the media.

Pastor Mary Bailey was leading James Foster around the room and introducing him to the church members at each table. When she stopped at our table we all introduced ourselves.

"You must know my old friend Alex Tate?" I asked.

"He was one of the founders of the South American Physician Volunteers."

"Of course," said James. "He is still very active in the organization. He spends six weeks every year with us." Harry Kahill nodded at Foster

"I see him from time to time." I replied. "He still has an office in Concord."

"We really need to get ready for the service," said Mary and hustled James Foster out of the parish hall. We all got up from the table. I went to the choir room to put on my robe, and the others went to take their places in the pews.

Ron Sinclair was playing the prelude on the organ as the choir gathered in the back of the church, ready for the procession down the main aisle. We had our robes on and our music scores out waiting for the processional hymn. As the prelude ended, Mary Bailey asked if there were any announcements to be made. We all looked at each other and sighed as we saw people lining up to speak. It's not that the announcements were not important, because they were. Each church group had information to give to the congregation. It was just the fact that most people take way too long to talk. One especially long-winded speaker went on and on.

By the time the announcements were over, most of us were ready to go home, but then the processional hymn started and we marched down the aisle singing. Once we were seated in the choir stalls and the opening meditation

Murder in the Choir Room

was said, we noticed that Reverend James Foster was missing. Mary Bailey signaled to Deacon Jane Foley to go find him, no doubt lost in the mazes of offices in the back. Most of the congregation was unaware of anything amiss, but we in the choir had a great view of the action. Mary Bailey got up to say the words of welcome.

"I want to welcome you all to All Souls' Church. We are a liberal religious community in the congregational style of worship. Whoever you are and wherever you are on your spiritual journey you are welcome here..." Suddenly a loud scream broke out from somewhere in the church, and the place erupted into chaos.

In the back hallway of the church there is an old lithograph from the early 1900's of Jesus on a fishing boat with his disciples. The waves and the wind are threatening to overturn the boat. All the disciples are in panic mode and Jesus calmly lifts his hands to stop the storm. There are times in life when amid panic and chaos one hero steps forward and takes charge of the situation. Unfortunately, this was not one of those times!

When Jane Foley let out a second scream, half the congregation sat in stunned silence and the other half jumped to their feet. Many ran out the back door and others rushed to the direction of the scream without any clear idea of where they were going. Tim, who had been sitting in the back of the church, was trying to make his way toward the office area behind the pulpit. He wasn't having much luck getting through the confusion.

Mary Bailey stood firm in the middle of the church trying to be a reassuring presence and continue with the service while the deacons and ushers dealt with whatever emergency was happening. Most people were ignoring her in the confusion. I left the choir stalls with the other choir members and we ran to the choir room. Luckily this time there was no body in the choir room, but then we heard another scream come from the pastor's office.

In the doorway of the office was Dr. Harry Kahill checking the vital signs of James Foster.

"He must have fallen and hit his head on Mary's desk. I've called 911 and they are on the way. It looks like severe head trauma," said Dr. Kahill.

"Jane, are you okay?" I asked. Jane Foley was sitting in a chair looking very shaken up.

"Thank God Dr. Kahill found him first. I was afraid there had been another attack. I screamed when I saw him on the floor. I didn't see Dr. Kahill at first," she offered.

"I was over by the window calling for an ambulance on my cell phone," explained Harry Kahill.

Just then Tim arrived and we filled him in.

"I'll wait with Harry for the ambulance to arrive. Jane, you need to go and reassure the congregation that it was just an accident and have Mary continue with the service as best she can," suggested Tim.

Somehow we all made it through the service, but everyone's nerves were shot.

Murder in the Choir Room

It was a frosty morning and a thin layer of ice that had formed in the puddles by the side of the road. The fog was rolling in from the river because the air temperature had dropped lower than the river temperature. November was on its way. It was already late October, and I had a lot to do before Jason and Monica's wedding.

"What are you doing?" I asked Tim as I stepped into the kitchen. Argus ran over to greet me, even though it had only been half an hour since Tim had gotten up and taken Argus outside.

"I'm having coffee and a slice of apple pie for breakfast," answered Tim.

"With a hunk of cheese?"

"Naturally!"

"You are," I said," such a Maine boy!"

"I saved you a slice," offered Tim.

"Thanks, any word about our accident victim?"

"I just called the hospital. James Foster is awake, but doesn't remember anything. He apparently is suffering from a concussion."

"Well, at least he's going to be fine. Can you imagine what it would be like if it had been another attack?" I said.

"What are the chances of an accident like that after what the church has already been through with the murder?"

"An unhappy coincidence I think."

"And I'm not even close to cracking the first attack

yet," said Tim. "What are you going to do today?"

"I'm going to spend the day making a wedding cake. If it turns out okay, I'm going to freeze it. If it doesn't, it's going on the compost pile. I need to give myself plenty of time to do it since I've never really done one before.

"I'm sure it will be fine. You are such a kitchen whiz."

"How about you?" I asked. "I see you're wearing your official uniform for public appearances."

"I need to do some official investigation. First, I need to check up on the leads you *found* when you were over to Billy's. Then I need to track down any leads I can get about Jack Riley's mysterious business trips."

"So when am I seeing you again?" I asked.

"I'm not sure how the day is going to go. I'll call you later and let you know." Tim gave me a squeeze and was out the door.

I had two layers of wedding cake cooling on the rack when the phone rang. I checked the caller ID before picking up the receiver and saw that it was Mary Bailey.

"Hello," I answered. "This is Jesse."

"Hi, Jesse, it's Mary, I'm calling because I'm going in to visit Jimmy Foster at the hospital and you're on the visiting committee. Are you able to come?"

"Sure Mary. I was just working on Jason and Monica's wedding cake. It needs to cool for a while, so I have some time free."

Murder in the Choir Room

"Great, I'll pick you up in about a half hour or so."

"Okay, I'll see you soon," and I hung up the phone.

On the ride to the hospital we talked about the effect of the murder of Jack Riley and Jim Foster's accident on the church. People's nerves were not good and everyone was uneasy thinking a killer could be among the congregation. Tim had tried to hint to everyone that the murder was probably a random act and had nothing to do with the church at all. Mary appreciated his efforts, but wasn't so sure it was working.

"I hope we can find justice for Jack Riley's killer and peace for the congregation," summed up Mary Bailey's hopes on the subject.

"At least once we know something for sure then healing can begin," I offered. Mary pulled her SUV into the parking lot and we entered the hospital.

"The last time I was in a hospital was when Jason was shot," I said. "I hate these places."

"Oh, Jesse, just remember this is a place of healing and hope for many who come here. It's not always a place of death."

"You are such a half-glass-full person," I remarked. "And I mean that as a compliment!"

"I'll take it as one," she said as we reached the door to Jim's room.

"Hi Jesse! Hi Mary, Mr. Foster is doing much better, and I'm sending him home on the plane tomorrow," said Dr.

Kahill who was just checking Jim's pulse when we entered the room.

"Thanks for the update Harry. Jim, this is Jesse Ashworth from the choir. You met him yesterday, but I doubt you remember much." Said Mary as she looked down at him on the bed.

"Thanks for coming. I don't remember much of anything from yesterday. Sorry to be such a bother and ruin your Sunday," he said from the bed.

"Don't worry about our Sunday," I said. "You're the one with the headache."

"He'll be fine," said Harry. "I have to go see to my other patients. Nice seeing you both."

"Bye, Harry," said Mary as he headed out the door.

"So are you going back to South America?" I asked. I couldn't envision such a long flight.

"I'm flying out to California for a few days and then back. It will break up the trip."

"Well, we should get going and let you rest. But I wanted to check on you and make sure you were okay," said Mary.

"Thanks. Take care both of you," he said as we headed out the door.

When I got back to Eagle's Nest the cakes were cool enough for me to work on. I made the mixture of sugar and water, sprayed the layers, and let it dry. This created a barrier that would keep the cake from crumbling as I applied the frosting. This was always the worst part for me. No matter how hard I tried I always got crumbs in the frosting.

The sugar water worked as well as it had on the earlier test cake, and I was able to get a good layer of frosting on the cake. It was beginning to look like a wedding cake. I added yellow trim to the white frosting and decided to stop there. It was pretty and simple, and if I added any more it would be spoiled. I boxed the cake up and made room in my freezer. Hopefully I would remember to take it out to thaw before the wedding!

"Smells good in here," greeted Tim as he walked through the door.

"Hi, I thought you were working today," I replied.

"Just taking a break. I sent out a watch for Billy Simpson's car. I got the license number from the state motor vehicle division and hopefully the car will turn up somewhere. I checked the hospitals and morgues and no unclaimed John Does have shown up."

"John Does? You sound like a TV cop!" I said.

"No shit! What's that great smell?"

"That is wedding cake. And for you to earn a piece, you will have to endure Monica and Jason's wedding."

"Endure? Hell, we have to be in it."

"So which one of us is the best man and which is the gentleman of honor?" I asked

"Does it matter?

"Not to me."

"Me either."

"Don't remind me! It's only a little more than a week away, and I've got to get cooking for the reception."

"I went with Mary to see Jim Foster," I said to get his attention.

"Did he remember anything?"

"Not a thing. Do you think it's important?" I asked.

"Maybe it wasn't an accident. Maybe it was another act of random violence. He's very lucky there was a doctor nearby or he could be much worse off."

"You think there is a killer on the loose in town?"

"It's possible, but I can't say so without sending the community into panic. I've put extra men on duty and there will be an officer at every church function."

"For how long?" I asked.

"Until I catch the killer."

Chapter 16

Today Viola was dressed in silver tights, and a loose silver sequined pullover. "Bright blessings, everyone!" Viola said as she entered the shop. The look of horror on Rhonda's face was worth the price of admission.

"You're in a good mood," I greeted her.

"It almost Halloween. It's like your Christmas for us Pagans."

"It's not really *my* Christmas" I said. I have never bought into the Christmas insanity. I noticed Rhonda had yet to recover. "And I thought Yule was the Pagan version of Christmas?"

"Yule is much quieter than Christmas, which is so commercial. For us Halloween is the big commercial holiday."

"I've noticed Internet sales have doubled over the past few weeks, and it's all been occult related sales. We haven't sold one plastic lighthouse," I said looking at Rhonda.

"There's nothing wrong with plastic lighthouses!" replied Rhonda, who had regained her speech. Today she was dressed in a 1970's peasant outfit.

"Plastic lighthouses sell well to little old ladies on tour busses. But Internet sales are different, and if you remember, you put me in charge of that part of your business." Rhonda was about to tell me to fuck off when a customer walked into the store.

"I'm here to get my fortune read!" said the

middle-aged lady. Viola took her into the corner of the shop behind the beaded curtain.

"I've got a fortune for her!" whispered Rhonda.

"And she's got fifty percent for you!" I reminded her. 'What the hell is wrong with you this morning. You're too old for PMS!"

"Low blood sugar, maybe."

I went to my desk and brought back the bag of applesauce muffins I had made that morning. "Maybe these will help?" Rhonda reached into the bag and took a muffin, gave it a sniff, and downed it in two bites.

"These are the best you've ever made!"

"Enough of this shit! Are you going to tell me what's wrong or not?" I could hear the shuffling of Tarot cards in the background as Viola was getting started.

"Jackson asked me to move in with him!"

"That's great! So what's the problem?" I asked.

"What would you say if Tim asked you to move in with him?"

"I'd say his house is way too small. Besides he stays at my house seventy percent of the time."

"Well," began Rhonda, "what if he expects me to do laundry, clean house, and cook? I'm not the least bit domestic."

"No shit! But this isn't 1950. Did you sit down and discuss this with him?"

"No."

"Do you want to live with him?"

"Yes," she replied.

"Well, sit down with him and talk about expectations," I said.

"I suppose that might be a good idea," she sighed.

I was about to give a sarcastic reply when the beaded curtains opened and the customer stepped out, thanked Viola, and gave her a ten-dollar bill.

"I want you to tell my fortune!" Rhonda said to Viola, and they both disappeared behind the beaded curtains.

Several hours later I was working at the computer when Rhonda came in with a bottle of Moxie in her hand and put it on my desk. I recognized the peace offering immediately. Argus got up and sniffed Rhonda's shoes. As soon as he was sure it was her, he wagged his tail. I looked at her and waited.

"The cards were right," she said.

"Okay," I replied in a noncommittal way. Argus recognized this as a break from work and jumped into my lap.

"The cards said I was afraid that I might repeat the mistakes of my past relationships and try to fit into a role I wasn't suited for. They advised me to break from the past and start over."

"And you needed a card reading to understand this?" I asked.

"I needed the reinforcement of a neutral observer," she replied.

"I see." Argus bored with the conversation, had fallen asleep in my lap.

"You should have your cards done," she advised.

"I don't want anything to do with Tarot cards," I replied.

"Really? Why?"

"I've found them to be too accurate. Every time I've tried to use them they've told the truth. The problem for me is they seem to always focus on the negative things in a reading. It usually reveals the things I fear. There is something negative about them."

"I'm surprised. I though you probably would think it was bunk," replied Rhonda.

"I always listen to my sixth sense and it tells me that they are not quite as harmless as they seem."

"And I've know you for over thirty years, and I'd trust you sixth sense any day."

After the walk home Argus and I sat on the back porch and watched the night settle in. It was a cozy place, now that Tim had put in the glass storm windows. I left the door open and the heat from the kitchen kept it warm. Several days ago I had given up and turned on the heat for good. Cold weather was coming and there was no escape.

"Jesse, are you here?" shouted Monica as she opened the front door.

"No, I've gone away to Florida for the winter," I said as she entered the back porch. Argus had run out to meet

Monica and was running circles around her as she walked toward me.

"Don't be an asshole," she said as she sat down.

"What's up?" I asked.

"I thought I would check in with you about the wedding plans," she said.

"And what else?" I asked. I had a feeling there was more to it than that.

"I know you are worried about Billy Simpson. I have the feeling that he is alive and okay somewhere."

"Is it just a feeling, or is there more to it than that?" I asked. She just gave me a look. "Okay," I admitted, "I have the same feeling. I think I would know if he were dead. I don't always trust my sixth sense."

"I know. That's why I thought if I felt it too, you might believe it."

"Maybe we should be on TV, like Psychic Detectives." I replied.

"We would need much more practice, I think."

"And more confidence. It's so hard to separate intuition from desire." I said.

"I know. It works best when it's something you don't really care about," said Monica.

"I've noticed that. Ironic isn't it?"

"For sure."

"Moving on," I said. "Let's finalize the wedding plans. How many people are actually going to be at the reception?"

"Including the wedding party, there will be twenty-two."

"Good, that should be easy enough. Flowers, church, everything is in order? No unpleasant last minute details I need to know?"

"It's a very simple mid-life second wedding. It shouldn't be a big deal," she said. I just rolled my eyes.

"Are Jeremy and Joshua coming?" I asked, referring to her two sons.

"Yes, and Anne and David are coming, too!" she answered naming Jason's two grown children.

"I haven't seen your kids since they were infants."

"Well, wait until you meet them. They are not tiny anymore."

"You mean they're tall?" I asked.

"Not exactly. Their father liked to eat and they inherited his appetite."

"I see," I said for lack of anything else to say.

"Come on," said Monica. "I'll treat you to dinner at Wong Ho's."

"It's a deal," I answered.

It was late and I was in bed reading a book. Argus was curled up on top of the comforter and taking up much of the bed. It had been a long day, and I was looking forward to finishing the latest best seller when the phone rang.

"I have some news," said Tim on the other end of the phone. I could hear voices in the background so I knew he was still at work.

"Is it good news?" I asked.

"I really don't know,"

"What is it?" I asked.

"We found Billy Simpson's car," said Tim. I knew there was more.

"And?"

"And Billy is nowhere to be found!"

Stephen E. Stanley

Chapter 17

It was Saturday, November second, All Souls' Day. The air was crisp and the skies sunny. In Western Christian cultures, All Souls' Day commemorates the dead. For our church, it is the day when the parish was founded in 1679. And today was also Monica and Jason's wedding day!

I had dropped off the wedding cake at the church earlier, so now I was making the lobster salad so it would be fresh. I scuttled the idea of Caesar salad and instead went with a simple Greek salad. The meatballs I had made yesterday looked pretty good, and I was fairly certain no one would notice that they really were made of soy protein and not animal flesh. By ten o'clock I had everything ready. The wedding wasn't until four, so I had some time to rest. At noon I took all the food over to the church hall and stored it away. I planned to put the hot food into warming trays and the cold food on ice right before the service, then change into my Sergeant Pepper tuxedo just before the wedding. Tim had the rings, so at least I only had to get myself upstairs to the wedding.

The rest of the morning and early afternoon, I relaxed and went over the list to make sure everything was okay. I figured I should fix myself up if I was going to be in a wedding. I knew that somewhere in my things I had a blow dryer, even though I hadn't used it since 1982. Usually I step out of the shower, comb my hair and forget about it. Today I put some goo in it, used the blow dryer and a comb, and gave it a little bit of style. I put on jeans and a tee shirt, packed the remaining food in the back of the Prius, took my Sergeant Pepper tuxedo with me, and headed to the church.

There was a lot of activity going on. The flowers were being brought in and the church was being set up for the wedding. I was alone in the parish hall. I brought out the wedding cake and placed it on a table that had been decorated especially for it. Rhonda had offered to set up the tables and decorate the hall, and she had done a great job! I put out the food, placing the salads on ice and the hot food in warming trays. I did a quick look around and then went into the men's room and changed into my tux.

After a few minutes of personal grooming, I decided that I had done the best I could and went to the parish hall to take one last look. I could hear a general buzz from upstairs and knew people had begun to arrive. I was ready to head upstairs when I heard Tim behind me.

"Hey Ashes I…" His voiced died away when I turned around to face him. He was looking very handsome in his tux. In fact I had never seen him so dressed up.

"What's the matter I asked?" I had never seen such a strange look on his face before.

"You… You… clean up real nice!" he said. 'I always thought you were good looking, but I never saw you like this." Maybe I should use the blow dryer more often.

"You're talking foolishness," I said. I was pleased, however. "You," I replied. "On the other hand look great, as always." Jason had entered unseen into the parish hall and was watching us.

"Hey, Newman and Redford, I need you both upstairs," said Jason. We both turned around. Jason also looked great in his tuxedo. I noticed too that he had a normal, understated tux, while Tim and I had the flashier fashions.

"Goulet, is there a reason you have us dressed up like bellboys?" asked Tim.

"I tried on those styles and they look great on you, but I am taller and heavier, and I looked like a stuffed bear." Just as he was speaking we heard the organ begin playing.

"Are you sure you're ready for this?" I asked Jason.

"As sure as I've ever been!" he said.

"Good answer. Now let's get upstairs," commanded Tim.

It was almost dark outside when the service began. Every window in the church held three candles and there were candles blazing everywhere. The front of the sanctuary was decked out with autumn colored flowers. The church looked warm and homey. Tim and Jason were waiting at the altar with Mary Bailey, who had on a festive clergy stole of white and gold.

Monica had a simple formal-cut gown of light blue with a matching hat. As man-of-honor I walked her down the aisle and passed her off to Jason. Tim and I stepped to one side. I'm not easily moved, but the service was lovely, and two very important people in my life were getting married. I admit that I shed tear or two.

Murder in the Choir Room

It all seemed to happen quickly and before I knew it we were all heading down to the parish hall for the reception. Monica's two sons, Jeremy and Joshua, moved up the reception line to meet me. Though Monica and I were close growing up, we had rarely corresponded as young adults, so I hadn't seen the boys since they were babies.

"It's nice to finally meet you Uncle Jesse," said Jeremy. "I've heard a lot about you."

"It's good to meet you too," I said. I didn't point out that we were really second cousins, since it didn't much matter.

"Uncle Jesse, we heard all the stories of you and mom growing up in a family that talked to ghosts," babbled Joshua when he met me. "It sounds really cool!" I really had a hard time telling them apart.

"So," I said to both of them, "what do you think of Jason?"

"I think they're great together, just look at them over there!" said one of them.

"She looks very happy, doesn't she?" asked the other one. I had to admit they both looked very happy. Just them Tim walked by with a plate of food.

"Great spread! I like the meatballs," he said.

"Actually they're veggie balls," I replied.

I grabbed some food and circulated around the room before sitting down at the head table with Tim and the newlyweds. Fortunately we skipped the speeches and toasts and simply ate and chatted. It was very informal and comfortable. Monica and Jason did cut the cake and there was a photographer discretely running around, but all and all it was enjoyable and relaxing.

"By the way," said Tim as he leaned over to me, "keep the tuxedo on until I get home." I was about to ask him why, but when I saw the look in his eye, I figured out why,

"No problem," I answered.

November's full moon, the beaver moon, was bright in the sky against the naked branches of the trees. The wind was gentle, but cold, and frost covered the bare ground. Though it was only four in the morning, I was wide awake, I got up and tip-toed out of the bedroom with Argus at my heels. I stopped and shut the bedroom door so as not to disturb Tim. I knew he had to get up in a few hours and probably work a double shift.

Jason and Monica had left on their honeymoon to Quebec City. I had suggested someplace warmer, but Monica, having spent the last thirty years with Jerry Twist in the deep South, said she had no reason to ever go south again.

After last night's wedding, I had stayed behind and cleaned up the buffet line, and I took the leftovers home and put them in the freezer. It always makes me a little sad to do clean up. Not that cleaning up makes me sad, but it was the realization that a time and place of happiness was over. Not to say there won't be other happy times, because of course there will be, but it will never be exactly the same again.

Murder in the Choir Room

I fed Argus, took him outside, and then made some coffee. I took a cup of coffee, wrapped myself up in a blanket in the chair, and settled down with Argus to read until Tim got up. I fell asleep thinking about Billy Simpson and awoke with a start sometime later as Tim came into the room.

"Where did you tell me you found Billy's car?" I asked.

"At the long-term parking lot at the train station in Portland. And good morning to you too!" he added.

"Sorry," I apologized. "I just woke up from a dream. The coffee is already on, and I took some waffles out of the freezer."

"Your so called dreams are sometimes scary," said Tim referring to my ability to sometimes clarify ideas during sleep.

"Any reason to believe that a criminal would steal Billy's car and leave it in a commuter parking lot? Wouldn't it be easier to just abandon it someplace more remote?"

"It's hard to say. Sometimes common sense doesn't apply to criminal activities."

"I guess you're right," I agreed. "So what are you doing today?"

"I have a few leads on Jack Riley's murder," he said.

"You have? How come I haven't heard about this yet?" I asked.

"Because you have a way of getting in the middle of my investigations and getting in trouble."

"Like what?" I asked.

"Well, let me think. How about the way you 'found' open letters on Billy Simpson's front porch? Or how about tracking down a killer who was planning on shooting you because you were too nosey? Do I need to go on?" asked Tim.

"Asshole!" I muttered. I hate it when he's right.

"And what are you doing today?" asked Tim to change the subject.

"I'm going to find Billy Simpson!"

"Shit!" was all Tim could say.

Chapter 18

The Sagadahoc nursing home was on the outskirts of town, nestled into the pine forests of North Bath. It once had been a home for the poor, but it had taken on a new life in the late 1960s and was now a home for the elderly. The morning had turned rainy, and it was cold and damp. I gave Argus a good brushing and packed him into the Prius.

I had been visiting the nursing home once a month or so for the past year. Argus seemed to sense the loneliness of the residents and loved the attention that the elderly gave him. My high school English teacher, Beatrice Lafond, had outlived most of her friends and family, so I took it upon myself to visit her now and again with Argus. When I reached the reception area, I put Argus down and he ran toward Mrs. Lafond's room.

"Well, Jesse. I figured Argus didn't get here by himself. Sit down." Argus was already sitting in her lap and getting attention.

"How are you Mrs. Lafond?" I asked.

"I'm on this side of the lawn, so I guess I'm doing okay," she said as she smiled. "And how are you doing?" She asked.

"Well, I'm worried about Billy Simpson; he's disappeared." I said and I told her the whole story.

"People don't just disappear, Jesse Ashworth. He has to be somewhere. And where is Timmy?" she asked, using Tim Mallory's high school name.

"He's following some leads on the Riley murder."

"I heard he's retiring," she added. "Has he had much luck on the case?"

"Not really," I answered. "It seems slow going."

"Of course it's slow going! Jesse, use your head! He's taking his time because he really doesn't want to retire. He thinks if he moves slowly, time will move slowly too. He's retiring because you're retired and he wants to spend more time with you."

"You really think so?" I asked.

"I've told you before, I'm old….."

"…not stupid," I finished the sentence for her. She says that every time I question her about something. Argus was watching us talk , and his head kept moving like he was watching a ping pong game.

"And I'll tell you something else, since it's right under your nose and you can't see it."

"What's that, Mrs. Lafond?"

"I know where Billy Simpson is!"

I just stared at her in disbelief!

It was night fall by the time I got home with Argus. The night was cold and the sky was clear. There were flashes of lightening on the horizon, as Argus and I settled in a chair on the back porch to watch the stars. The lightening had a green cast to it and began to intensify. As the colors began to change, I realized that the season was too late for thunder storms and that I was a witness to the northern lights!

Argus, curled up in my lap, could have cared less

about the heavenly light show. I had seen the aurora borealis many times when I was a kid, but not as an adult. We are often so busy living day to day that we forget to look up at the sky and consider the universe.

As I watched the celestial light show, I replayed the events of the day. When Mrs. Lafond told me where Billy Simpson was, I couldn't believe that I hadn't figured it out. Old lady Lafond always had a soft spot for the dull-witted students in her class, and she often treated me as one. She patiently took me step by step through the information I gave her until I discovered it myself. Billy had recently divorced his wife under less than ideal conditions, he was depressed, and when he was at my house recently, he drank way too much. Rehab! Billy Simpson wasn't missing; he was at rehab!

"And think, Jesse, if his car was in Portland, where did he go for rehab?"

"To Boston?" I asked. His car was at the long term parking lot of the bus station.

"And why wouldn't he drive to Boston, if that were the case? Isn't the station also used for local busses?" she asked.

"I guess so," I said, feeling like the dim-witted child.

"And if the rehab center were in the outskirts of town, wouldn't it have a parking lot?" she asked.

"I guess so,"

"So that must mean that the rehab center is in Portland. Do you think that might narrow it down?" she asked in the same tone of voice she used on me in high school.

"How is it you were able to figure this out and I wasn't?" I asked. I was really irritated with myself.

"I told you before, I'm…"

"Don't say it!" I said. Then I went over and gave her a kiss on the cheek and headed home with Argus in tow.

A quick web search told me that there was only one alcohol rehabilitation facility in downtown Portland. I also knew that if I called they wouldn't give me any information as to who was or was not there. I grabbed Argus and put him in the car and drove to Portland. The Kramer Rehabilitation Center was located on a quiet street across from a small city park. I found a parking spot on the street with a view of the center, and staked out the area to see what I could see.

Argus was getting restless, so I took him into the park to do his business and to give him some water. We were sitting on a bench when I saw the door open and a group of men and women leave the center and head toward the park. I knew if Billy was there he would spot me, and having Argus with me would be a dead giveaway. I quickly picked up the pug and ran behind the bushes out of sight.

When I didn't see Billy, I stepped out from the bushes and then I spotted him at the end of the line. I quickly ran back to the bushes, jumped behind them, and tried to hide. Outside the bushes I saw a pair of black shoes. When I looked up I saw that the black shoes were attached to a police officer!

"Something I can help you with?" he asked.

"No, sir. Just walking my dog," I replied. He looked at me suspiciously.

"There's been some drug dealing and prostitution going on in this park, so be careful." He was watching me for a reaction. I slipped my free hand into my coat pocket and felt for my key fob. I pressed what I hoped was the alarm button.

"That's my car alarm!" I said. "Somebody must be breaking in." I was hoping to distract him and it worked. I ran over to the car and looked it over. The police officer followed me.

"Doesn't seem to have been anything," he said. He looked at the Prius. "Have a good evening," He walked away. I guess Prius drivers for the most part aren't into major crimes.

The northern lights had taken on the appearance of luminous draperies hanging in the sky. It was getting chilly on the porch, but I didn't want to leave the light show. Argus, who had been fast asleep, raised his head and ran for the front door. I knew Tim had arrived, though I wasn't expecting him. I heard the front door unlock and Tim stepped out to the porch.

"I stopped by to tell you about the northern lights, but I see I didn't need to," he said.

"Thanks, they are spectacular! Sit down. You want a beer?"

"Hell, yes," he answered. "I had a busy day."

"Any movement on the Jack Riley case?"

"His latest credit card statements arrived by mail, and his wife turned them over to me. We have a lead on his latest business trip. Seems be just spent a week at Lake Placid before he was killed. He attended some charity convention. And what did you do today?" he asked to be funny. "Bake cookies or nap all afternoon."

"I did neither," I shot him my killer look. "In fact, while you were fucking off at the police department. I found Billy Simpson!" I walked into the kitchen to get Tim a beer and left him with his mouth still open.

Murder in the Choir Room

Chapter 19

Jane Foley, the most senior member of the board of deacons,was the chair of the committee. "Last year, as you all remember, we had a very successful Thanksgiving dinner here at the church. We were able to have dinner with many of our church family and guests from the community who might not have had anywhere else to go."

It was true. Thanksgiving had been one of our best community outreach programs. Many single persons and empty-nesters from our church, along with some families, shared a great thanksgiving meal in the church. Those who were able brought homemade dishes for the meal. We had donations of turkey and ham which I helped cook in the church kitchen. We invited many from the community who were down on their luck. We even had enough food to send leftovers home with everyone.

"The way the economy is going, I expect we'll have even more this year," said Rhonda, who always kept up with the latest economic news.

"I have no objections to working on a Thanksgiving dinner again. I'm sure Rhonda would love to be the main organizer again," I said. Rhonda shot me a look. "And I'll cook the main dishes. And it was great last year when people brought their favorite dishes to share."

"Last year was wonderful," chimed in Mary Bailey. "You all worked very hard."

"Thanks!" replied Betty Chase, who hadn't done a blessed thing but show up.

"I'm sure Betty would love to be in charge of this year's clean up!" said Rhonda with an evil smile.

"That's wonderful!" said Mary Bailey picking up on the theme. "Thank you for volunteering."

"I'd be happy to do it," said Betty who hadn't volunteered and was not happy at all to do it either.

We spent another hour doing our planning, which in any other group but a church group could have been wrapped up in ten minutes. Rhonda and I headed back to Eagle's Nest for a light supper.

"Thanks asshole for volunteering me to run it!" said Rhonda when we were out of earshot.

"I figured you could get rid of some more of your store's junk as center pieces," I answered.

"I don't sell junk!"

"And that's why you have all those leftover plastic light houses. And you did a good job nailing Betty Chase, by the way!"

"She's a pompous twit!"

"The worse kind!"

She drove me back home where Argus gave her a warm greeting. I made bean sandwiches for our supper. I toasted two slices of bread, put on some farm-raised cooked bacon slices, covered them with baked beans, sprinkled on some grated cheese and placed them under the broiler until the cheese bubbled and turned slightly brown. We each had a bottle of Sea Dog Ale.

"So where's Jackson?" I asked. "I haven't seen your

boyfriend in several days."

"He's visiting his kids."

"And when are you two heading north for a vacation?"

"As soon as I think I can leave Viola alone in the store for a few days."

"She's fine," I said. "You really don't have to worry. And Brad can help out; he's been with you for more than a year. Don't be such a control freak,"

"And where is Tim?" she asked.

"Tim is in Bangor visiting his daughter at the university."

"Any progress on the Riley murder?"

"I went to see Mrs. Lafond. She thinks Tim is dragging the case out because he doesn't want to retire."

"Makes sense to me," said Rhonda. "And what about Bill Simpson? Has he solved that one?"

"Actually," I answered. "I solved that one," And then I told her about how Old Lady Lafond got me to figure that out. "I've only told you and Tim. We should probably keep it quiet and respect Billy's privacy."

"Excellent idea! When are Jason and Monica due back?"

"Sometime next week, I believe."

"Do you think they're doing it?" asked Rhonda with a wicked smile as she took another drink.

"Do bears shit in the woods?"

Stephen E. Stanley

It seems that no matter how many projects I finish, or how many loose ends I tie up, there is always something more to do. I used to get really annoyed with friends who were recently retired and would say "I'm busier now than when I was working. I don't know where my time goes." I always wanted to bitch-slap them, but now I was turning into one of them. I really think the human condition is to stay busy and fill up the days.

I had just finished up Jason and Monica's wedding, and now had to plan for the church Thanksgiving. I achieved very little progress on my cookbook, and I was probably behind in filling orders at Erebus. In addition I needed to prepare the gardens for winter, rake up the remaining fallen leaves, clean the house, start Christmas shopping, and any number of other things.

None of these things was going to get done today, however. I was taking the day off. I harnessed Argus up and we went for a walk. It was cool and brisk and felt good to be out and around. My neighbors were all out raking leaves. I waved to the Lowells as I went by and waved to Beth White who was scraping frost off her windshield.

"Hi Beth, settling in okay?"

"So far, so good! I'm not happy about the frost!"

"Welcome to Maine," I said. Argus and I turned the corner and headed down the street to town. The frost was evident on all the parked cars along the way. There was a slight fog on the river because the air temperature was cooler than the water temperature. Being out and about I felt a little better and decided to do some work at Erebus. Viola was working.

"Good morning, Jesse! Hello Argus," said Viola as I entered the shop. Argus was jumping up and giving Viola licks. Today she was dressed in a skirt and blouse of army camouflage.

"Nice dress," I said. "I can barely see you!"

"Oh, Jesse, you are a hoot!"

"Is the old bitty in?" I asked. "I didn't seen Rhonda's car outside anywhere."

"She called this morning and asked if I could open. She seemed a little agitated."

"Oh, good! Just what we need!" I couldn't think what had agitated Rhonda, as I had just seen her last night and she was fine.

"Well, better she's at home if she is agitated," responded Viola.

"Amen to that," I answered. "Could you look after Argus for a few minutes? I'll go to the coffee shop and get us some coffee?"

"No problem, Jesse," she answered.

I walked down the street to the coffee shop. Brian Stillwater was behind the counter. We exchanged greetings and I got two coffees to go. Brian was dressed in his usual Native American accoutrements.

"I'm planning on beginning the spiritual discussion group next week. Can you make it?"

"Sure, and I have a few people to bring, too."

"Great, should be fun. Have a great day," he said and turned to wait on some other costumers, most of whom looked like they needed an immediate caffeine fix.

When I got back to the office and turned on the computer, I was sorry I had come in. The orders were waiting, and they would take me nearly the whole morning to process. I was going to have to hit up Rhonda for a raise pretty soon. Argus spent the morning following Viola around the shop and then hiding and sleeping under my desk.

By noon I had finished the orders and was about to close up when I felt a presence in the room and looked up.

"I thought you were still in Bangor," I said to Tim as he stood in the doorway.

"Just got back this morning. Jessica is coming home for Thanksgiving."

"That's great!" I said. Jessica had spent last Thanksgiving with friends. Even though he said it was fine at the time, I think he was disappointed.

"Do you think the Lowells would watch Argus for a few days?" Argus has been sleeping, but when he heard his name he jumped up and rushed over to Tim.

"I'm sure they would," I answered. "Why?"

"We're going to Lake Placid!" said Tim

"Lake Placid?"

"Jack Riley's last business trip was to Lake Placid, New York. I thought I would do a little investigating and mix business with pleasure."

Murder in the Choir Room

"I'm in! When are we going?"
"Tomorrow morning!"

Chapter 20

There was a dusting of snow on the ground when we arrived in Lake Placid. It looked like it had been there for a while. It also looked like the town was gearing up for the winter sports season. We parked the car and checked into the resort. Our room had a great view of Mirror Lake and the Mountains beyond. We headed into the bar to unwind and have lunch

"This is nice! Very scenic," said Tim as he looked at the view of the village and lake.

"Yes, it is. I've been here before and liked it very much. So what are we going to do?"

"Jack Riley made a donation to the Global Neighbors Fund, which has its headquarters here. He also attended a conference here just before he died. I thought I could do some investigating and we could also have some down time."

"This is the first time we've actually gone away together," I observed. We both ordered a pale ale from a local brewery.

"Yes, it is," replied Tim with a smile. "But it won't be the last time!"

"I'm still having trouble picturing Jack Riley as a doer of good deeds. He was such an asshole to everyone in Bath. Even Reverend Bailey found it hard to find anything nice to say about him at the funeral."

"Not to mention," added Tim, "that his wife broke into hysterical laughter at the eulogy when someone said something nice about him."

We read over the menu and both ordered the grilled trout with wild mushroom rice, accompanied by baked squash. The food was excellent and we both ate in silence. As the plates were cleared away, we ordered coffee.

"The weather is great and we have the whole afternoon ahead of us," I said. "What are we doing first: business or pleasure?"

"It's chilly out, but sunny. Let's go bundle up and head out for a walk through the village. We'll stop at the Global Neighbors' office and then walk around Mirror Lake. If it's not too far, that is."

"The walk is two point seven miles around the lake," I said.

"How do you know that?" Tim asked.

"Just a piece of trivia I remembered. Now if you ask me what I had for breakfast, I couldn't tell you," I replied. Tim just nodded.

We headed back to our room and dressed for the weather. Though it was sunny, there were clouds gathering by the mountains, and the weather people were calling for snow later. We headed into the village and since it was between seasons, there was very little activity. We found the Global Neighbors' office on the third floor above a sports shop in the center of town.

A young woman was sitting at the reception desk when we walked in. Tim showed her his badge and asked to see the person in charge.

Stephen E. Stanley

"That would be Mrs. Bancroft. She is the regional director of the program." She disappeared into the office and returned with a middle-aged African American woman in a rather severe business suit.

"What can I do for you Chief Mallory and …?" she looked at me.

"This is my collogue, Dr. Ashworth," said Tim. I gave him a sideways look. I never use my academic title. Tim must be trying to impress.

"A pleasure, Dr. Ashworth," she said as she shook my hand.

"We are looking into the murder of Jack Riley. He made a rather large donation to your organization recently and traveled up here for a conference shortly before he died," Tim said as Mrs. Bancroft took us into her office and indicated that we should sit at the small conference table.

"I see," she said. "Let me get out the files for you." She went to the file cabinet, picked up a red file folder and handed it to Tim.

"Jesus Christ!" said Tim after briefly looking over the folder.

"Exactly," replied Mrs. Bancroft. Tim handed the file folder over to me.

"My, my, this is interesting!" I said as I looked over the file. It appeared that Jack Riley wrote out a big check that his bank could not cover. The check bounced.

"That's only half the story," continued Mrs. Bancroft. "Jack Riley was on our board of directors and had access to our funds. Most of our money goes to medical assistance in South America. Apparently only half the money we sent arrived at its destination."

"So Jack was ripping your organization off?" said Tim. It wasn't really a question.

"I'm afraid he was," Mrs. Bancroft replied.

"Did you report it to the authorities?" I asked.

"We've only just discovered the discrepancy during an outside audit."

"So you haven't yet reported it?" asked Tim. I noticed that he was taking notes.

"No. We will as soon as the audit is finished."

"Did Jack know that your organization was going to be audited?" I asked.

"It was in our annual report, which went out in late October."

"Jack was already dead when that came out," Tim observed. "Thanks for your time. You've been most helpful. If you think of anything else give me a call." Tim gave her his card.

"I certainly will." She got up and walked us to the door.

I noticed the receptionist checking out Tim as we walked out of the office.

"What do you think?" asked Tim as we walked out of the building and up the street.

"I think the receptionist would like you to interrogate her."

Stephen E. Stanley

"I meant about the interview, asshole."

"I think that everyone is justified to think that Jack Riley was scum. Stealing from charity? That very well might be the motive for murder," I replied.

"Money is always a motive. I think we need to look much closer at Jack Riley and his charity works."

The rest of the day we spent sightseeing by taking a drive out in the Adirondacks. The sky was a brilliant blue and really emphasized the snow covered mountains. Skiers were already on the slopes thanks to the cold weather and the ability of modern technology to create snow.

We returned to the village and found a great little Italian restaurant for dinner. Then we went to an ice skating completion at the ice arena.

"I'm not sure I get what they are trying to do," said Tim as we watched the skaters glide and loop over the ice.

"Looks lovely, though, doesn't it?" I replied as a male skater in a tight costume jumped and twisted.

"Yes, yes it does," answered Tim.

On the drive back the next day we took the ferry across Lake Champlain. It was very cold and we stayed in the ferry's cabin where it was warm and dry. We arrived in Burlington and crossed Vermont into New Hampshire and then back to Maine. I was anxious to get home and pick up Argus. I knew the Lowells would take good care of him, but this was one of the few times he had spent the night without me.

Murder in the Choir Room

It was after dark when we pulled into the Lowells' driveway. I could hear Argus barking as I went up the steps.

"How did he do?" I asked Dorothy Lowell.

"He was fine. He sat in my lap all day and then slept on the bed all night. He does seem glad to see you, though" she said. That was an understatement. Argus was jumping on me and barking and then running to Tim and barking and going back and forth.

"Thanks so much for looking after him," I said as I handed her a wrapped package. I had bought them two Adirondack mugs.

"Anytime," said John. "He was no trouble at all, and he was great company."

"Did you learn anything from your trip?" asked Dorothy.

"Oh, yes," answered Tim. "More than we wanted to know. But as usual, the more answers you get, the more questions that pop up."

"And that," stated John, "is what makes life interesting."

"This happened to you last year, too," said Dr. Kahill as he took the thermometer out of my mouth. "As soon as you close the windows for the season, you develop allergies."

"I know," I said. "But it's too cold for fresh air this time of year."

"That's why you need to come in and get a prescription for allergy medicine."

Stephen E. Stanley

I was sitting on the edge of the examining table. Since coming back from Lake Placid, I had been stuffed up and uncomfortable.

"I thought people had allergies during the spring and fall," I said.

"They do! And some, like you for instance, are sensitive to indoor pollution. Try to spend more time outdoors when you feel stuffed up."

"I will," I promised.

"Anything new on the Jack Riley murder?" he asked.

"Not that I know of," I answered. I wasn't at liberty to discuss what Tim and I found out about Jack Riley in Lake Placid.

"Not to speak ill of the dead, but we shouldn't be wasting tax dollars looking for Jack Riley's killer. Jack was a nasty piece of shit."

"That," I said, "seems to be the general feeling about him."

"Now go get this filled and get some fresh air. And let me know if Tim makes any more progress on the case."

"I will," I said as I left the doctor's office.

Chapter 21

Rob Sinclair was waving his arms in the air. "I know it's not Thanksgiving yet, but we need to be thinking about Christmas music for Christmas Eve." We all groaned. Choir rehearsal was once again well-attended. I wasn't sure I could sing well because of my allergies, but I would try.

"Is it going to be a long service?" asked Karen Fulbright, a soprano. Karen was new to the church.

"In the age of short attention spans," answered Rob, "any service over an hour and fifteen minutes would be risky."

"Any special music you have in mind, yet," I asked.

"I thought we could do something with Medieval Celtic music. Something new that people won't be familiar with."

"Great idea!" observed Ben Bailey, tenor and Mary Bailey's adult son. "People will be so sick of canned Christmas carols by then,"

"Yes,' replied Rob. "I was thinking of having a whole theme for the music portion."

Suddenly the fire alarm in the church went off. We all hesitated and looked at each other before we headed to the nearest exit. Fortunately we were all New Englanders and we grabbed our coats on the way out, which was a good thing considering that it seemed about one hundred twenty-five degrees below zero outside.

"Hopefully, it's just a false alarm," said Rob.

"Most likely," I said and then we all saw it; a figure

- 167 -

in a black hooded sweatshirt running out the back of the church. Three of us took off after the figure, but he had a head start and since we were all of middle years, we had to give up the chase.

Two fire trucks pulled up and firemen in combat gear went through the church looking for fire. Tim pulled up in a police car just after the fire trucks arrived. Harry Kahill appeared shortly after that.

"I was on my way back from the hospital when I saw the fire trucks and thought I might be needed," Dr. Kahill said to me.

"I don't think anyone was hurt, but it's great of you to stop to help," I replied. I liked Harry Kahill because he was always ready to help.

"Are you okay?" Tim asked when he made his way over to me.

"I'm fine," I replied. Then I told him what had happened. Just as I finished we saw two firefighters running into the building with a hose.

"You stay here," said Tim. "I have to check this out."

We all huddled together in the cold and the dark hoping the damage wasn't too bad. We saw the firefighters return with the hose, so the fire must have been very small. One of Tim's officers arrived and took down our statements. There really wasn't much we could tell him. None of us got a good look at him, or her for that matter. After a while Tim returned. In his hand he had a black hooded sweatshirt.

"I found this in the bushes down the street," he said.

Murder in the Choir Room

"Whoever did this thought he might be recognized."

"Any damage to the church?" I asked.

"There was a small fire set in the steeple. It did very little damage. I've sent a description of the intruder, based on the description you people have given. I've contacted the pastor and I think it best if you all go home now."

We all turned to walk away.

"All except you," Tim said to me. "You always have a way of being in the middle of everything. Let's go out for a snack."

"Sure thing chief," I replied.

The morning sky was red as I got up. My grandmother used to say "Red sky at morning, sailor take warning." The air felt like a storm was coming and Argus, not a fan of cold weather, only stayed out long enough to do his business and then scrambled back into the house. I was planning an "at home day." I needed to work on my long-neglected cook book. I built a fire and settled myself at the kitchen table with my recipe collection.

Tim was working the day shift and was planning to come for dinner. I'm sure with the church fire and all, he hadn't gotten to bed until early morning. Sifting through the recipes, I found lots of material for the cookbook and found an interesting recipe for vegetable lasagna that I decided to use for dinner.

"Jesse, are you here?" yelled a voice as someone opened my front door. Argus ran off to check out the

Stephen E. Stanley

intruder.

"In the kitchen. Come on in!" I recognized the visitor as Jason Goulet. "Back from your honeymoon I see."

"It feels strange to be married again, even though we've been together for a year."

"And how was Canada?" I asked.

"It was cold, but Quebec was very nice, and the food was unbelievable."

"Storm's coming," I said. "I think we might be in for a big one."

"Monica's out shopping to stock the pantry now, just in case. She sends her love and says she'll check in with you later. What's up for Thanksgiving?"

"Just the same as last year." I told him about repeating the church-wide Thanksgiving dinner.

"Any word from Billy Simpson?" Jason asked.

"I haven't heard a thing from him," I said, which was true. I left out the fact that I had hunted him down. "I have a feeling he will show up soon."

"How about Jack Riley's case?"

"Well, that seems to be going slower than I expected." I then told him about old lady Lafond's theory that Tim was trying to delay his retirement.

"That makes sense. Maybe we need to talk to him."

"You may be right, but there has been some movement." And I told him about Jack taking money from charities.

"Are you kidding me? No wonder someone wanted

to kill him."

"That's the problem," I replied. "Everyone wanted to kill him."

"Oh, before I forget, we brought you something from Quebec," he said as he handed me a package.

When I opened it, I found a church cookbook from St. Peter's Parish in Drummondville, Quebec. I've collected church cookbooks for years. Nobody has better recipes than church ladies!

"Wow, thanks," I said. "And it's in English, too!"

"I figured that would help!"

After Jason excused himself and drove away, the sky became very dark and a driving rain started. I threw another log on the fire and started putting ingredients into the bread maker. Next I boiled the lasagna noodles and layered the dish and had it ready to put in the oven before Tim got here. I still had a few hours left so I settled myself on the sofa with a book. Argus, who loves a good fire, had established himself in front of the parlor stove and was napping by the fire.

I must have fallen asleep, because the next thing I knew the bread machine was beeping to let me know that the bread was ready. I let the bread cool on a rack and put the lasagna in the oven. Argus had seated himself in the living room by the front door. It was a sure sign that Tim was on his way. I never could figure out how Argus knew in advance, but he always seemed to know when someone was coming. Most dog owners have noticed their best friends' uncanny abilities.

Stephen E. Stanley

In less than ten minutes Argus started to bark and I knew Tim had arrived. I went to the kitchen and grabbed a bottle of beer from the fridge and passed it to him as he took off his wet coat.

"Something smells good. I didn't stop for lunch and now I'm starving."

"Still raining hard, I see."

"It's worse than that. It's freezing rain."

"I'll get the lantern out then." Freezing rain in a bad storm usually means a loss of electricity, sometimes for days.

"I stopped at Trash Mart and bought some fresh batteries," said Tim as he pointed to the bag he had left by the door.

"Thanks, we may need them. Go sit by the fire and dry out; I'll get dinner ready."

"With pleasure," he said as he threw another log on the fire.

I brought dinner out on a tray so we could eat by the fire.

"Anything new on the Riley case?" I asked.

"I spent the morning going over the reports. One thing struck me as odd."

"What's that?" I asked.

"That nobody saw anything unusual, and yet Jack Riley left the service early with the plate offerings and ended up dead in a section of the church that he had no business being in."

Murder in the Choir Room

"I've been thinking," I said. "The fact that no one saw anything unusual probably means whoever did it must have belonged there. That indicates whoever did it is most likely someone we know."

"Let's review all the stuff that's happened in the last few months, even if it doesn't seem related," said Tim in between bites of food.

"Wait, I'll get my note cards and add to the list," I offered. I ran into the kitchen and grabbed some recipe cards and a pencil.

"Let's start over," began Tim. "Jack Riley was killed by a brick doorstop in the choir room of the church. It was not his turn to take the collection, but he did. He took the collection from the sanctuary earlier than was the custom. Bill Simpson was the lead usher who gave him the offerings. Billy has since disappeared and gone into rehab."

"We need to look at Jack Riley, too," I added. "He was a church trustee and trustees work with the church's money. Jack was a school board member and co-owner of a software business. He and the other co-owner did not get along. In general everyone hated Jack Riley. Jack also took business trips that have turned out to be trips to charitable events. As it turns out he has been ripping off one group that we know of so far. There are no shortages of people with motives."

"His funeral was well-attended," broke in Tim after a few minutes of silence. "But no one seemed to be out of place there at all. It was a week after he was killed that you noticed the door to the steeple was open and we found the murder weapon wrapped in a choir robe."

"That's always bothered me," I said."Why didn't someone discover it earlier? Do you think someone planted it there days later?"

"I think that's a very real possibility."

"Then whoever planted the brick and the robe had access to the church."

"I'll check with the church office," Tim said. "But I think the church is unlocked most of the time."

"I've been thinking. James Foster hit his head in the church on Sunday morning. Is it possible he was attacked by the same person?"

"Anything is possible, I suppose," replied Tim. "But he was a guest preacher and I can't think of any motive since no one here knew him. Nothing was taken so robbery can't be a motive."

"What if Dr. Kahill scared off the attacker?"

"Maybe, but unlikely."

"Okay," I thought I'd take a different angle. "There were robberies in town and it turned out to be Jack Riley's nephew."

"You're trying too hard," Tim replied. "Usually it the simplest answers that lead to the truth."

"The truth is," I sighed. "We really don't have any clues at all."

Chapter 22

It was evening and the coffee shop was closed to the public. Brian Stillwater had directed us to enter by the back door. The smell of freshly brewed coffee greeted us as we entered. It was the perfect spot for a meeting.

I brought Monica, Viola, and Beth White with me. That added two who were raised as Spiritualists, as well as a Jew, and a Pagan to the group. Brian was a follower of Native American spirituality. In addition there were two Buddhists, a Unitarian, and two Episcopalians. If nothing else we were a very diverse group.

"Thank you all for coming," began Brian. "It has long been my dream to establish a group of seekers from different spiritual paths to share fellowship and understanding. That being said, we should probably have some basic ground rules. Any ideas?"

"How about," began Beth White, "All religions are valid paths to God."

"I have an issue with the word God," said Tom Sewall, the Unitarian.

"Okay," replied Beth. "All religions are valid spiritual journeys?" There were no further objections and we adopted the statement.

"When we speak," I suggested, "we speak only for ourselves."

"Good point," observed Brian. "I think those rules are all we need. Help yourselves to coffee and cookies, and let's get started."

Stephen E. Stanley

We each introduced ourselves and gave a brief account of our spiritual backgrounds. Most people had little knowledge of Spiritualism, thinking that it was just a group of people gathered around the Ouija board. Monica explained that it was really an organized denomination that was essentially free of creeds and rules, and though most followers believed that we could communicate with the dead, it was really an admission that there is more to life than can be seen with the eyes. I added that Monica and I were still free-thinkers, but not totally convinced about life after death.

Beth gave us a brief account of Reform Judaism, and we peppered her with questions. Viola's Pagan background was one of the most entertaining, since we all had preconceived notions about witchcraft and Halloween.

We were so involved in our conversations that at first we didn't see the two police officers at the front doors. We were all startled when then began banging on the door to get our attention, Brian went to let them in.

"Dr. Ashworth, would you come with us please?" said the taller of the two. I recognized both of them, but couldn't remember their names.

"What is it?" I asked.

"It's Chief Mallory. He's been taken to the hospital!"

There is a certain smell that the autumn nights have that is hard to describe. The air is cold and crisp and fresh smelling. Anyone who has grown up in the Northeast would recognize it instantly. I was shivering in the back of the police cruiser as we sped through the night on the way to the hospital. I'm sure it was fear and not the cold that was making me shiver.

"Tell me again what happened, Sergeant Bates?" I had remembered the two officers' names, but I couldn't focus on what they were saying.

"I went into the chief's office and found him slumped over his desk. I called the paramedics and they took him away; then I came to find you."

"Thanks," I said automatically. For all I knew Tim could have either passed out from fatigue, been shot by a perpetrator or had cardiac arrest.

The ride to the hospital seemed endless, though I'm sure it was no more than ten minutes. Jeff Bates had the lights flashing and the siren blaring. Any other time I would have enjoyed the ride. When we arrived at the emergency entrance, I tried to jump out of the police car, but the doors had no handles. I had to wait for Officer Johnson to open it for me.

"Sorry," he said. "It's a security feature in case we are transporting criminals. We can't have them jumping out of the car."

I ran into the hospital and asked the nurse at the desk about Tim.

"Are you a family member?" asked the nurse, eyeing me with suspicion.

"Yes, he is," said Sergeant Bates, who had stepped up behind me. "Now answer his question. This is police business."

I shot Jeff Bates a grateful look.

"He was brought in with an irregular heartbeat. He's being treated by Dr. Goldring. Have a seat and I'll have him come out."

I sat down in the waiting area with the two uniformed cops on either side of me. I must have looked like a sick criminal. I didn't care. About forty minutes later, a guy in a white jacket came out and introduced himself as Dr. Goldring.

"He's been asking for you Dr. Ashworth," he said as he led us down a long hallway.

"How is he, Dr. Goldring?" I asked.

"He'll be fine, though I want to keep him here for a day or two for testing. He had an irregular heartbeat and passed out. We need to find out what caused it, though."

"Any ideas?" I asked.

"Does he do any drugs?"

"No! I've never seen him so much as take an aspirin," I replied.

"Well, I've taken some blood samples to check. It is possible that he ingested something. Of course it could be just about anything, including a bad heart. But he's strong and everything seems fine." He broke off as we entered the hospital room. Tim looked pale, but smiled as we all entered.

"You look like hell, Mallory," said Bates.

"Trying to get out of work?" asked Officer Johnson.

"Are you okay?" I asked.

Murder in the Choir Room

"Relax everyone, I feel fine, now," Tim said.

"You can take him home tomorrow," said Dr. Goldring to me. "If his tests come back normal, he can go back to work in a few days. Until then he needs plenty of rest."

"Hey," said Tim. "You're talking about me like I'm not here."

"Never mind him," I said to the doctor. "I'll make him rest if he knows what's good for him."

"Well chief," said Sergeant Bates. "Unlike you, we have to get back to work. Take care of yourself and don't worry about anything." Both officers waved and were gone.

"Don't," Tim turned to me, "call Jessica. I don't want her coming home from school early. She'll be here for Thanksgiving next week anyway. I'll tell her then. No need to alarm her for nothing."

Just then Monica came through the door. Tim assured us both that he felt fine and not to worry. Monica offered me a ride home.

"I'll be back in the morning," I said. "And don't ever scare me like this again."

The sun was shining through the windows on the back porch, warming the area with solar heat. Argus was curled up in Tim's lap as Tim sipped on a cup of herb tea.

"I'm fine. You don't have to wait on me," objected Tim.

"You are not fine. You had an irregular heart beat

Stephen E. Stanley

and you passed out. So just sit back, relax, and stop bitching."

"Hard ass!" said Tim.

"If you want something to do," I said passing Tim the phone, "call everyone and tell them you're okay. It's better if they hear it from you."

"I'm fine. I could go home and take care of myself you know."

"And I could call your daughter Jessica and tell her what happened."

"Blackmail?" Tim asked.

"You bet your ass!"

Tim sighed and started calling everyone. I left him and went into the kitchen to work on my cookbook.

Chapter 23

It was five in the morning of Thanksgiving Day. I was in the church kitchen and the turkeys were already in the oven. The church ladies would be arriving soon to set up the parish hall and help with the side dishes. I was making out a schedule for all the volunteers to follow. Last year everything had gone smoothly and with any luck this year would be even better.

My sixth sense was acting up, and I was pretty certain something was up today, but other than a vague feeling of uncertainty, I hadn't a clue what was coming. That vague feeling of change, that nagging voice in the back of my mind, I call "The Distant Thunder," and today it was thundering.

I wasn't surprised when I felt a presence in the kitchen, but was shocked when I turned around and saw Billy Simpson standing there. I ran over and gave him a hug.

"What are you doing here?" I asked.

"I read your request for help in the church's online newsletter, so I'm here to help!"

"I could use an extra hand."

"I've been in rehab, as you well know. I saw you hiding in the bushes that day. I should have known you'd find me."

"You could have told us where you were. We were worried."

"It was morning and I had just about scraped bottom. I called the rehab place and they said to come in immediately. So I left everything and drove to Portland. Honestly, I was in such a bad place I was sure no one would even miss me."

"Well, we did miss you!" I said. I didn't say that it took us several weeks to realize he was missing. "And I could really use your help. Here's a checklist. Would you mind taking inventory and see if we have everything?"

"Sure thing!" he said and went about the task.

By noon the church ladies had everything under control. I'm convinced that church ladies are the backbone of every church community. These women are hard workers with kind hearts and no nonsense attitudes. Betsy Wallace, Emma Smith, and Florence Goodwin were my chief helpers. They worked efficiently and skillfully preparing the side dishes. Other church members brought in their favorite dishes to share and we had more food than we knew what to do with. Here was the parable of the loaves and fishes come to life.

As we had last year, we put out a general invitation to the community. Anyone who was alone, or had fallen on hard times, or who simply wanted to be with others was welcome. Thanksgiving was for sharing.

By one o'clock people began to arrive. Dinner was scheduled for two, but we were running behind so we put out appetizers and planned for two-thirty. Tim was much better and had gone back to work. He was planning to join us unless there was an emergency.

Finally everything was ready and Mary Bailey

started the festivities "Welcome to All Souls Church and our annual Thanksgiving dinner. We are honored by you presence here with us today. Whoever you are and wherever you are on life's journey, you are welcome here. I want to give thanks today for the hard work of Rhonda Shepard, Jesse Ashworth, Emma Smith, Florence Goodwin, Betsy Wallace, and the whole Thanksgiving committee of All Souls for their planning and dedication. Now I'd like to invite Rabbi Beth White to lead us in a Thanksgiving prayer."

Beth stood up and prayed:
"Great God of all,
Let us give thanks for the joy
Of gathering together for this community blessing.
We give thanks for the food
Prepared by devoted hands.
We give thanks for all the blessings of life,
And the freedom to enjoy it all."

I looked around and saw that we had nearly double the number of guests from last year.

"Jesse is going to tell us about the good food we have," said Mary Bailey.

"We have farm-raised turkey, naturally cured ham, and a vegetarian Thanksgiving loaf. We also have stuffing, mashed potatoes, squash, carrots, peas, turnips, and corn. All the vegetables are organic and locally grown. Our coffee and tea are fair trade. We have many side dishes and desserts too numerous to name and prepared by many of our guests, but there are labels for each. Please help yourselves as we have more than enough food!"

For a moment nobody moved and then in one great moment everyone lined up for the buffet. The church ladies, Rhonda, and I were the last to line up. There was the great sound of people talking, but it began to get quiet as people began to eat. Rhonda and I sat with Tim, his daughter Jessica, Jackson Bennett, Monica and Jason, and Billy Simpson. Billy took the opportunity to tell us all about his stint in rehab. Bill certainly looked better and seemed more at ease. Monica and Jason talked about their honeymoon in Canada, and Jackson told us of his plans to expand his insurance office.

"Something's been bothering me. I've been thinking about the day Jack Riley was murdered," said Billy out of nowhere. "As you know I was the head usher that day. Being in rehab gave me some time to think. I remember seeing someone get up and head in the direction of the choir room before the end of the service."

"Did you see who it was?" asked Tim.

"Yes, it was Mark Anderson."

"The principal of the high school?" I asked.

"Yes, it was him," said Bill. We all took a moment to take in this new information.

"But he really wouldn't have a motive," I added.

"Actually" said Jackson quietly, "now this is just a rumor, but you know David Hackett who works for me is on the school board?"

"Oh, yes," replied Jason. "I know him. We were on the basketball team together."

"Well," continued Jackson, "according to him, Jack Riley wanted to fire Mark and claimed he had evidence of wrong-doing."

"Mr. Anderson was a great principal," interjected Jessica. "I'm sure there was no wrong-doing."

"Did he ever say what evidence he had?" I asked Jackson.

"No. But I understand he gave Mark an ultimatum; resign or be fired."

"And that," said Tim, "would be a motive."

"I may commit murder myself," said Monica, "If you men continue to talk business on Thanksgiving."

"And I'll gladly be an accomplice," added Rhonda.

"Yes, captain!" said Tim with a salute.

"Do you think my father will be okay with retirement?" asked Jessica Mallory. She was sitting at my kitchen table slicing up a dozen oranges.

"I can't see him getting up in the morning, having a cup of coffee, and that's it for the day," I replied. I told her about my suggestion that he open his own security and inquiry office.

"You mean become a private detective?"

"Something like that; though I'm sure it's not like it is on television."

Stephen E. Stanley

"Well," said Jessica, "I think it's a great idea. Maybe I could even work for my father when I get my criminal justice degree." She handed me the cut up oranges that I placed in a pot with lots of sugar.

"I'll bet he'll like that," I replied. Jessica smiled.

"How do you make cooking look so easy?" she asked. "It always seems to be a big deal for me."

"The secret," I said, "is that I only cook when I want to. I make big batches and freeze lots of food. When I don't feel like cooking, I run to the freezer. I also eat out a lot. The result is that I only cook when I feel like it. If I had to feed a family of four three times a day, it would be a full time job."

"So what are you going to do with all this home-made marmalade?" she asked as I filled the dish washer with jelly jars to sanitize.

"Christmas presents. Everyone gets fruitcake and I wanted to be different. I'm putting together homemade marmalade in a basket with scones. It makes a great Christmas breakfast."

"Do you think Mr. Anderson had anything to do with Mr. Riley's death? He was a great principal. I can't imagine him as a killer."

"I don't think rumors and speculation can be considered evidence at this point." I answered. "Your father will know more about it." Just then we both heard Tim drive up and park. "And here he is!"

"Hi guys! What's up?" asked Tim. He gave me a squeeze and walked over to Jessica, kissed her on the top of her head and sat down at the table. I poured him a cup of coffee.

"I'm helping Jesse make orange marmalade."

"Good. You'll make someone a good wife someday."

"In your dreams, Dad." Jessica and Tim had a running joke going. Jessica, at age twenty, declared marriage an outdated form of female slavery. Tim smiled.

"I'm having coffee with David Hackett, the school board member later this morning. You two want to come along?"

"The one who told Jackson about Jack Riley wanting to fire Mark Anderson?" I asked.

"That's the one."

"Sure, but isn't it a little unusual to have civilians at a questioning?" I said.

"Yes, but I want to give the impression that this is not an official investigation, but just a social event."

"That's great Dad!" Jessica beamed at her father.

"And," added Tim, "I'm chief of police and I can do anything I want!"

"We've noticed!" said Jessica as she winked at me.

Brian Stillwater brought four coffees to our table and set them down. "I hope you realize that not everyone here gets table service!"

"Thanks Brian," I said. "It never hurts to be nice to the chief of police. You never know when you might need a parking ticket fixed."

"Whatever!" said Brian as he walked away.

"How's everything going?" Tim asked Dave Hackett.

"I'm expecting my first grandchild around Christmas," replied Dave.

"It's always a shock to me," I said, "when someone in our generation becomes a grandparent."

"That's something I don't mind waiting for," said Tim. Jessica just rolled her eyes.

"So what am I really here for?" asked David.

"I just wanted to check some information I've heard," replied Tim. He gave David a brief report about what we had heard from Jackson. "Needless to say, we don't want to jump to any conclusions based on hearsay."

"I was at the school board meeting when Jack Riley demanded Mark Anderson's resignation. He accused Mark of wrong-doing, but he wouldn't say what it was."

"So he did ask for Mark's resignation?" I asked.

"Yes, but Mark refused and without any basis to fire him, we voted to table the action pending any proven allegations."

"I see," said Tim without expression.

"So you have no idea what the allegations were that Jack accused Mr. Anderson of?" asked Jessica.

"None at all," he replied.

"Is it possible that Jack made the whole thing up?" I asked.

"It's possible, I suppose. But it was Mark's reaction that was interesting?"

"How so?" asked Tim.

"Well," began David, "it seems to me if there were no truth to it Mark, would have been angry and defensive. Instead, he looked a little shaken and just got up and left the room."

We all looked at each other for a moment. Tim asked David if there was anything to add. There wasn't and David excused himself. Jessica, Tim, and I finished our coffee.

"It's all very interesting, but there is no solid evidence to link Mark Anderson to the murder. All we have is some unsubstantiated accusations which would never hold up in court," said Tim.

"You really don't think Mr. Anderson is a murderer, do you Dad?" asked Jessica

"Everyone who knew Jack Riley is a suspect," replied Tim as he downed the last sip of his coffee.

Chapter 24

The cold air and the warmer river water temperature had created an early morning fog that cloaked the downtown area in an eerie light. It would be several hours before the sun could burn through and dissipate the fog. I had made a batch of donut muffins to take to the shop. Tim was spending his time with his daughter, and though I understood the father and daughter bond, I was feeling a little left out.

Argus was walking beside me sniffing everything in sight. I still walked to work, but when the snow came later in the month, I would have to drive to town. After all, Argus didn't like to get his feet cold.

I was early and opened up the shop. I turned on my computer and made a pot of coffee. When the coffee was ready I poured out a cup and began working on the internet orders. Sales had picked up as we got closer to Christmas. Rhonda was coming in this morning to begin decorating the store for the holidays, but we both agreed to keep it simple. There was to be no canned Christmas music. In fact I had vowed to go ballistic if I heard "Jingle Bell Rock" one more time.

Rhonda came in the front door dressed in a vintage 1920's outfit, complete with cloche hat. The skirt was very short.

"Are you showing off your legs or just airing out your lady parts?" I asked.

"Asshole!"

"Donut muffin?" I offered.

Murder in the Choir Room

"You bet your ass!" We settled in the back room with coffee and muffins. "What's new with you?"

I gave her a brief outline of my life for the past few days. Before I could finish, the front door opened.

"Bright Blessings, everyone!" Viola had arrived, and I could swear that Rhonda cringed. She was wearing a red turban on her head with a bright blue and red peasant dress, along with the ever-present silver jewelry.

"I really need to find my own fashion expression," I muttered.

"What's with him?" asked Viola pointing at me.

"He's grumpy today. Pay him no mind," replied Rhonda.

Viola grabbed a deck of cards and put them down in front of me. "Cut the deck," she said. I did as I was told. "Now cut the deck again and turn over the top card." I turned over the card. It was the nine of cups.

"This is a very good card. This is the card of happiness and plenty! You are blessed!" said Viola as she picked up the card.

"So stop your fretting and count your blessings, and get to work!" added Rhonda.

"Okay, okay!" I said. I went back to my desk and worked on orders. When I had finished that, I updated the web pages on the store's site to reflect the holiday season. After a few hours Argus was getting restless, indicating a need for a walk and a potty. Just as we stepped outside, Tim was coming down the street.

"How about some coffee?" he asked. "I'll go into the coffee shop and get take out."

"Pick up some sandwiches and we can make it a lunch," I answered. "I'm starving."

"Sounds good. I'll meet you on the water front."

Argus and I walked down the hill to the small river park. It was very cold, but since restaurants don't allow dogs, it was our only dining option. Tim rolled up in his police car and brought our sandwiches over to the bench. Argus took up his spot under the bench while we ate.

"You're quiet today," stated Tim as he looked at me.

"Don't mind me. I can feel winter approaching with its short days and long dark nights."

"How's the cookbook coming?" Tim asked.

"I'm almost done. I should be able to mail it off to my agent next week."

"How is Rhonda's sister, by the way?"

"She's doing well in the agent business, according to Rhonda. She also has a new love interest in her life."

"Hasn't she been married before?" he asked.

"Four times at last count, if I remember correctly."

"Chief Mallory?" We turned around to see a teenage girl standing behind us."

"I'm chief Mallory," said Tim to the girl.

"I went to the police station to see you and they said I could find you here."

"What can I do for you?" asked Tim. The girl seemed frightened.

"I need help," replied the girl and looked at me. Something was really wrong.

"This is my friend Dr. Ashworth. You can trust him. Come and sit down and talk to me," said Tim kindly to the girl. She bent down to pat Argus, who jumped up to give her a kiss. "What's your name?"

"I'm Amanda Gilbert. I'm a senior at Morse High."

"Tell me what's happened." I'm always impressed with Tim as a cop. He can be tough as nails, or as in this case, kind and caring.

"I've been getting these emails," said the girl settling in between us with Argus in her lap.

"Take your time," Tim said. "This is Argus. He likes people."

"Hello, Argus" said the girl giving him a hug. She dug in her purse pulling out several pieces of paper and handed them to Tim. He read them slowly, then folded them up again.

"How long have you been getting these?"

"About every few weeks since school started."

"Has he ever approached you in person?" Tim asked.

"No, never. In fact I have the feeling that he doesn't even know who I am."

"Do your parents know about this?" Tim asked.

"No, I was afraid they might blame me for being on the Internet if they found out."

"May I keep these?" It wasn't really a request.

"Sure."

"Listen to me, Amanda. This is not your fault. I'm going to take care of this. I'll speak with your parents and then find out why you are getting these."

"Thank you," replied Amanda. Tim gave her a hug before she left.

"There are times," said Tim, "when I feel like I actually make a difference."

"Never doubt it," I answered. "So what was that all about?"

"Read these," Tim said as he passed them to me. I read them over.

"They are suggestive, but not obscene and not threatening."

"Take a closer look at the headings of the email," Tim suggested.

"Holy shit!" as I looked at the heading I could see that they appeared to be sent from the principal of the high school.

"The smoking gun we've been looking for."

The sun was shining brightly through the glass on my back porch. The solar radiation had heated the area to a warm, comfortable level. Argus had found a sunny spot on the floor and was keeping one eye on Monica and the other eye on me. He was trying to follow our conversation, but gave up and drifted off to sleep. Monica had come over to spend the afternoon with me. Tim and Jason would be joining us later

Murder in the Choir Room

for dinner.

"So, is the Jack Riley murder solved?" asked Monica.

"Not really. It does look like Jack was putting pressure on Mark Anderson to resign as principal. The suggestive emails were traced to Mark's office computer and it does give him a motive to kill Jack. Bill Simpson says he saw Mark leave his pew in church just before Jack was killed. The problem is the lack of physical evidence linking Mark to the Murder."

"What happens now?" asked Monica.

"Mark has been put on unpaid leave from the high school, pending an investigation into the emails. He hasn't been arrested, yet. But he has been named a person of interest. In reality, the news media have already convicted him."

"What's your gut feeling on this?" Monica asked.

"It's more than a gut feeling. Mark Anderson has been set up by someone. My sixth sense is screaming at me that this is wrong. Unfortunately, gut feelings are not admissible in court."

"And my gut feeling," replied Monica, "tells me that your gut feelings are correct. I hate knowing something and not having anybody believe me. People just nod at me and roll their eyes like I'm crazy, but not dangerous."

"You remember the Greek Myth of Cassandra?" I asked.

"Yes, the god Apollo gave her the gift of prophecy."

"And then he gave her the curse that no one would believe her."

"It's just like that, isn't it?" she asked.

"Yes, except I think we don't voice our feelings because we fear people will think we're whack jobs."

"Three hundred years ago they would have hanged us for being witches. Does Jason trust your intuition?"

"Yes, he does. How about Tim?"

"Tim trusts my sixth sense. Police Chief Mallory, however, wants physical evidence."

"So what are you going to do?" asked Monica

"I'm going to go with my gut feelings and assume that Mark Anderson is innocent."

"Need help?"

"I do, thanks!"

"So what's for dinner?" asked Monica to change the subject. At the word dinner, Argus woke up and sat at my feet.

"Chicken in the pan."

"Need any help?"

"Sure, I have an extra vegetable peeler somewhere."

The four of us sat in my kitchen, dining by candle light. The conversation had ranged from religion and politics to current events and recent movies. Good food, good wine, and good companions are some of the joys of life.

"Where's Jessica tonight?" asked Jason.

"She's out with some girl friends. They are having a

sleep over and also encouraged me not to come home tonight."

"Sounds like she is getting a life of her own," remarked Monica.

"She's twenty," sighed Tim. "What am I going to do?"

"She's a good kid," I said. "Whatever you did as a father, you need to let her go."

"She wants to be a cop," Tim replied. "I'm proud on one hand and really scared on the other."

"You're lucky," added Jason. "I see my kids once a year. They have their own lives now."

"I love my two sons," said Monica. "But they plan on staying in Georgia. At least they call once a week."

"Okay, you guys are really scaring me now," said Tim.

"Let's take our coffee into the living room," I suggested in order to change the subject. We all took seats by the fire. As soon as we moved from the table, Argus got up and led the way. He went to his cushion by the fire, circled three times, and settled down. The rest of us arranged ourselves in seats by the fire.

"How's the murder investigation going?" asked Jason.

"I think we have our guy," answered Tim referring to Mark Anderson. "But Jesse doesn't think so."

"I agree with Jesse," added Monica. "But it's just a feeling."

Stephen E. Stanley

"Unfortunately, feelings are not admissible in court," stated Tim. Just as he said it the hairs on the back of my head stood up and I shivered involuntarily. I looked over at Monica and could tell she felt something too.

"Tim, there's one or two missing pieces in this puzzle. I think you need to go back and look for something you missed." Monica was nodding her head as I said it.

"Any ideas where I should start?" asked Tim.

"There is something terribly, terribly wrong," answered Monica. "This is a giant web that covers more than what you realize. You shake one area of the web and the vibrations will be felt over a great area. There is great danger."

We all looked at Monica like she had lost her mind. Then I looked at her eyes. I had seen that look on my grandmother several times and grandmother was never wrong. No one said a word for a few moments.

"Sorry," said Monica. "I don't know why I said that. It just came out."

"Well," said Tim. "It might be a good idea to retrace the investigation. It couldn't hurt." Tim knew about our family history and looked a little shaken.

Chapter 25

The darkness was impenetrable. It was early morning, and I sat in the kitchen with a cup of coffee. I had taken Argus out to do his morning business and after I fed him, he ran back into the bedroom and snuggled down on the bed with the sleeping Tim Mallory. I'm a light sleeper and usually only average six hours a night. Tim on the other hand can sleep anywhere at any time.

Slowly the sky lightened up with streaks of gray and pink, and then a brilliant red sunrise. It was seven in the morning and the sun was just getting up. Winter was going to be dark and long. Tim stumbled into the kitchen with Argus trailing behind him. I could see the creases in Tim's face where the pillow had left marks.

"What's up today?" Tim asked.

"It's Sunday. You are taking me to breakfast before church. I'm singing in the choir, and then Billy Simpson, Jackson Bennett, and Jason Goulet are coming over to watch the game," I said as I poured Tim a cup of coffee and refilled my own. "And you are not going in to work, no matter what!"

"A day off! It's going to be great!"

I wasn't so sure.

December sunlight was coming through the church windows. It was the first Sunday of Advent and the first candle in the advent wreath was burning. The choir would be singing, "O Come, O Come Emmanuel" as the Sunday

- 199 -

anthem. Tim was sitting with Jessica in the back of the church. I watched as Tim pulled his cell phone out of his pocket, looked at it and then left the church. I knew he had left orders that he was only to be contacted in an emergency. What emergency could there be on a Sunday morning?

I tried to concentrate on the Bible readings, but I was watching the back of the church for Tim's return. Finally I saw Tim return to his seat. I could tell from his body language that he had learned something, but since he returned to the church service, I deduced it wasn't an emergency that needed his immediate attention.

It was probably my imagination, but the sermon and prayers seemed to go on way too long. I was anxious to know what Tim's phone call was about. Maybe it's just that I'm nosey, but I couldn't get out of my choir robe fast enough.

"What was the phone call about? You never take cell phone calls in church."

"Work stuff," answered Tim. I knew he was playing with me.

"Okay," I said, playing along. I knew he was dying to tell me.

"You remember Irene Bancroft?"

"We meet her in Lake Placid. She was the head of Global Neighbors," I answered.

"Well, I just got a courtesy call from the Lake Placid Police. Irene has been arrested for embezzlement."

"What?"

Murder in the Choir Room

"She tried to blame Jack Riley for the missing money. The investigation revealed that she had transferred the missing money to an offshore bank account."

"Do you think it's tied into Jack Riley's death?"

"There's more," added Tim.

"Of course there is." I was getting confused.

"The account was in the Grand Cayman Islands, and Jack Riley had taken several business trips there."

"And...?" I knew there was more.

"And, he had access to the account. We found the account number among his personal papers. We didn't know what the account numbers were until now."

"Do you think that she might be involved in Jack's murder?"

"It seems like a possibility."

"What about Mark Anderson?" I asked.

"That's the problem," answered Tim. "We have too many suspects at the moment. And for all I know, there may be others."

"I doubt there will be any more suspects after two months," I said.

As it turned out, I was wrong.

There was a dusting of snow on the ground as Argus ran around the yard. Each year Argus acts like he's never seen snow before. He puts his nose down on the ground, sniffs the snow and runs around the yard like he is possessed. I knew it wouldn't last long. After about three minutes he sat down, lifted his paw and looked for me to pick him up. Pugs hate the heat, hate being wet, and hate cold feet. On a really cold day, he can do his morning business in less than one minute.

The sky was clear and the snow would be gone by mid morning. Sometimes the upper air is so cold that the moisture in the air freezes and falls without a cloud in sight.

I called Rhonda and told her I wasn't going into Erebus this morning. I was close to finishing the cookbook and wanted to get it in the mail by evening. She wished me good luck. I told her I'd catch up with her later.

I spent the morning typing out the last of the recipes. The task seemed overwhelming at first, but as I worked along, coming up with vegetarian dishes became easier. It took a lot more creativity to make tasty dishes, but compared to the few cuts of meat that make up most meals, the variety of fruits and vegetables was vast.

By noon I had the cookbook finished and emailed it to Janet Shepard, my agent, who was also Rhonda's sister. It was very handy to have your best friend's sister as an agent. It gave me a slight edge in the market. I knew I'd hear from her by the end of the day.

The house keeping fairies had once again failed to appear, and I spent the rest of the afternoon scraping soap scum off the shower stall walls, scrubbing toilets, vacuuming floors and dusting bookcases. The last task of the day was cleaning the French cook stove. Since it was enamel and cast iron it wasn't all that hard to clean. Tim had promised to take Jessica and me out for dinner, so I didn't have to cook anything today. By the time I was finished puttering, it was time to go for dinner.

"You know, Dad," said Jessica over a streaming bowl of fried rice. "I really like having the house to myself."

"You don't like having me around?" asked Tim looking crushed.

"I love having you around," continued Jessica. "It's just that I like sleeping late and staying up late and eating when I want. And I also know that you like to stay at Eagle's Nest with Jesse. What I'm trying to say is that you don't have to change your routine for me. If you want to stay at Jesse's, then stay. I know where I can find you."

"You are a good kid," I said. Jessica rewarded me with a smile.

"I got a warrant to search Mark Anderson's office," said Tim changing the subject that was clearly making him uncomfortable.

"I don't think he did it, Dad."

"I don't think so either," I added sipping my tea.

"Well I have officer Murphy checking his computer. If there's anything, there she will find it. She is one of the best computer geeks I have."

"So what's his status?" I asked.

"Right now he is a person of interest," said Tim biting into a spring roll.

"What about Irene Bancroft of Lake Placid?" I asked.

"Lake Placid PD is checking her alibi."

"You need to slow down, Tim. You don't want to have another attack."

"What attack?" asked Jessica.

"Oops!" I thought Tim had told her about it.

"It was nothing," replied Tim. "One minute I was having coffee with Harry Kahill and then when I got back to my office I felt dizzy. It was no big deal."

I disagreed, however I thought it in my best interest not to pursue it any further.

"Maybe you can't be left on your own," said Jessica eyeing her father.

"You just worry about your grades," replied Tim. "And I'll deal with you later," he said looking at me.

"Sex addict," I answered. Jessica burst out laughing, much to Tim's discomfort.

Fortunately the bill arrived and distracted us from the current conversation. Tim grabbed the bill out of my hand and paid it.

"Thanks for dinner Dad. I'll plan on having the house to myself tonight." Jessica gave her father a kiss, me a wave, and sailed out the door.

"She's all grown up," I observed.

"Apparently," sighed Tim.

Even though it was morning, it was dark outside. I could hear the rain beating on the roof and I snuggled down into bed and closed my eyes. Tim and Argus were snoring away and I had no desire to start the day in the dark. It was December and we were heading to the darkest time of year. I wasn't happy. I don't mind the cold. In fact I like cold, sunny days, but I hate the dark. When the world becomes dim at four in the afternoon, I go around the house and turn on every light, but it doesn't really help.

"Where's breakfast?" asked Tim as he nudged me in the back.

"At Ruby's, if you're lucky," I answered. Tim knew my dislike of making breakfast.

"Grumpy, aren't we," said Tim. "If you get dressed I'll buy you breakfast."

"Okay," I said. "What are you doing today?"

"I'm going in to work and see if Jan Murphy has had any luck with Mark Anderson's computer. You want to come along?"

"Sure beats what I had planned." I actually had no plans at all for the day. No need to tell the big guy, though.

The sun was up by the time we finished breakfast at Ruby's. The waitress was being very attentive and spent most of her time flirting with Tim. I felt invisible and not for the first time.

"Looking on the bright side," I said between bites of scrambled eggs, "at least I get good table service when I'm with you, even if the servers never give me eye contact."

"It's the uniform," explained Tim.

"You're not wearing your uniform," I replied.

"So I'm not," he answered grinning.

Officer Janet Murphy had her blonde head bent over the keyboard as we entered the police station. She looked up, gave us a greeting, and went back to hitting keys.

"I've found something interesting," she remarked.

"What is it?" I asked.

"Well, for one thing, I checked the email files. There is no evidence that he sent those emails from his school account."

"Could he have deleted them?" asked Tim.

"Yes, but deleting them only removes the file name from the hard drive. It tells the computer that the files can be written over, but in most cases deleted files can be recovered. I'll try recovering them next."

"What else?" I asked. Janet hit a few more keys and brought up some images. We looked at them.

"These were in a file folder on his computer desk top. No attempt to file them away. It certainly is risky for him to have them on his office computer.

We looked as she scanned through the photos. There were images of women in various stages of undress.

"Tasteless," remarked Tim. "But not illegal."

"But certainly against school district policy," I added.

"There's more," said Janet. She reached into a file folder and brought out the hard copies of the emails that the teenage girl had given Tim. "Though these appear to be from

Mark Anderson, they did not, in fact, come from this computer."

"How do you know?" Tim asked. Janet just gave him a look.

"Because you pay me to know things like that. For one thing, the routing of the emails is different. The sender was clever enough to try and make them look like they came from Mark's computer, but they were sent from a totally different account. Whoever sent these is a good computer hacker. But not," she added, "as good as me."

"What about the pictures?" I asked.

"All someone had to do was get in the office for five minutes, plug in a thumb drive, and download the pictures to Mark's desktop."

"It still could be a motive for murder. If Jack Riley knew about the files and threatened Mark, it would be a motive for murder."

"Just one problem with that Boss," said officer Murphy. "The creation date of these photos was two days after the school board suspended Mark. I'm pretty confident that he is not your suspect."

Chapter 26

The phone rang early the next morning. I checked the caller ID before answering it. It was Rhonda's sister, AKA my book agent.

"I am not," I said into the phone, "posing for any illustrations!" Janice talked me into posing for photos for my first cookbook. When it came out it was full of pictures of me cooking in a run-down trailer kitchen. I was nicknamed "The White Trash Cook."

"Really, Jesse, get a grip! I'll line up illustrators for the new book. I think it will do okay. I just called to tell you that your publisher has accepted it and will begin working on it. You should get the galley proofs in a few weeks. And I'm fine, thanks for asking."

"Oh!" I said. Maybe I had over reacted. "How are you doing?"

"My new hubby is wonderful. And rich," she added. "When is what's his name going to marry my sister?"

"His name is Jackson, and I think it's Rhonda who is gun shy and not him."

"I never could tell her anything," she sighed. "I'll email you when the proofs are ready." She rang off.

With no cookbook to work on, and no Erebus scheduled until late afternoon, I was using the day to get caught up on things. I was working on a long shopping list of provisions for the pantry in case of a three-day storm. I had several loads of laundry to do, and I thought I should string up the white Christmas lights outside the house.

Murder in the Choir Room

I try to avoid the Christmas insanity as much as possible. My contribution to the season is a one-foot Christmas tree in the living room and white lights strung around the front porch. I avoid stores and restaurants that play canned Christmas music. The candlelight Christmas Eve service and Christmas dinner with friends is the total of my holiday. It's enough.

The day was surprisingly warm in the fifties, and Argus and I were outside. He was sitting and watching me balance on the step ladder draping lights over the bushes and along the porch railings. I connected them to a timer and tested the lights. Everything was working. I would keep the lights going until New Years Day, when I would, hopefully, be able to take them down. Last year we had a severe ice storm and the Christmas lights were frozen solid until March.

I had just finished stringing the lights and was putting the step ladder away when Tim pulled into the driveway. Argus made a beeline to Tim, barking all the way.

"Hey," I said. "What's new?"

"We just cleared Mark Anderson. The school board is going to meet tonight and re-instate him as principal."

"That's good news," I replied. "But I don't suppose that gets you any closer to who really killed Jack Riley."

"No it doesn't. And now I have to find out who set up Mark Anderson and why."

"You think they are related?" I asked.

"Maybe, maybe not."

"Thanks for clarifying," I replied.

"It's what I do."

Rhonda had taken the day off and Viola was working until three when school got out and Brad Watkins would come in to work. It was the Christmas season and Erebus would be open until eight every night. Brad liked working at Erebus and enjoyed earning the extra money during the holiday season. It really didn't take two people to work the front of the shop, so I made myself busy in the back room at the computer. Internet sales were brisk and I had plenty to do getting the orders out before Christmas, which was just two weeks away.

"So what do Pagans do for the holidays?" I asked Viola when she came into the back room. Today she was dressed in blue jeans, white blouse, and a vest made out of faux fur. She was sporting lots of silver jewelry.

"It's the festival of Yule, the winter solstice. For us it's the return of the sun. Or looking at it another way, it's a turn of the wheel of the year. We decorate our homes with evergreen boughs because evergreens are a symbol of eternal life. We burn candles on the darkest day of the year to welcome the rebirth of the solar year. It is one of the oldest of holidays. Your church forebears couldn't stamp out the solstice celebrations, so they Christianized it."

"I've read," I replied, "that most biblical scholars believe that Jesus was born in the spring. Lambs are born in the spring and that's when shepherds would be attending their flocks."

"Now, take Halloween; there's a real holiday!"

Just then Brad Watkins came into the shop. "Hi Guys," he said as he hung up his coat.

"Hi Brad," said Viola. "Well, I guess it's time for me to hit the trail."

"I love the bumper sticker on your car!" replied Brad.

"What does it say?" I asked.

"My other car," answered Brad, "is a broomstick!"

The shop was busy and Brad had plenty to do working with the customers. It was dark outside and I was anxious to get home. Argus and I had walked to Erebus because it was a fairly warm day for December, but now it had turned cold after sunset.

"I'm going to wrap up here. Are you okay to close up?" I asked.

"No worries! I'm fine," answered Brad.

I was putting my coat on when I had a thought. "Do you know Amanda Gilbert?" Amanda had been the recipient of the emails alleged to be from Mark Anderson.

"Sure," said Brad. "She's a nice girl, but bad taste in men."

"How so?" I asked. Most teenage girls had bad taste in men.

"She's going out with Peter Thompson."

"The asshole who broke in here and stole the

atheme?"

"That's the one," answered Brad.

As soon as Argus and I stepped out of the shop, I flipped open my cell phone and called Tim.

I picked up the visitor pass at the front desk of the police station. Even though everyone here knew who I was, it was a good idea to follow protocol. Officer Janet Murphy led me into a back room with one-way glass so I could watch the interview with Amanda Gilbert. Tim joined me in the room along with Bath's juvenile advocate officer. Janet would be conducting the interview. Amanda was brought in and left to herself for a few minutes. She glanced at the mirror and rearranged her hair. Even though most people have seen TV interviews a hundred times, most of them never give a thought to whether the mirror is one way or not.

The three of us watched as Officer Janet began questioning Amada.

"Hi Amanda, I'm officer Murphy. I thought I might be able to help. Tell me about the emails." Amanda told Janet the same story she had told Tim and me at the waterfront park.

"What did you think of them?" asked Janet.

"I thought they were a bit creepy. We had learned about cyber stalking in school, but I was afraid that if I told my parents about the emails they wouldn't let me use my computer anymore."

"Did you really believe that they came from your

principal?"

"I did at first, but when I began to think about it, it didn't seem right."

"So, who did you think sent them?"

"I thought it was one of the girls in my class, but I didn't know who. That's when I went to see chief Mallory. I wasn't sure who sent them, but I was afraid."

"Do you believe her?" asked Tim. We were sipping coffee and watching the interview.

"Yes, I do. If she were lying, she would have used the same words to tell Janet what she told us. It would be like a script. She gave Janet the same information, but varied her words," I said.

"I think she's telling the truth, too," agreed the juvenile advocate officer, whose name I learned was Daniel.

"Is Peter Thompson your boyfriend?" asked Janet. Amada looked horrified.

"Oh my God, no," she replied emphatically."We went out once. He wasn't nice and I refused to go out with him again. Then he began spreading rumors that we were together, if you know what I mean."

Tim left the room and went into the interview room to thank Amada for her cooperation and to assure her she wasn't in trouble.

Once Amanda Gilbert was safely out of the police station, Peter Thompson was brought in. He was dressed in jeans and tee shirt with a jeans jacket. Tim left him in the interview room to cool his heels for a time. Peter whipped out a comb and ran it through his hair as he admired himself in the mirror. He straightened his collar and pointed at his image and winked.

"Charming," I said.

"Let's go," said Tim. He and Daniel went into the interview room, while Janet Murphy joined me for the observation.

"Are they going to do good cop, bad cop?" I asked.

"Watch and learn," she answered.

Tim and Daniel took turns grilling Peter. Peter used the bravado that only arrogant teenagers can use. He denied nothing. He admitted sending the emails to shake up Amanda and bragged about breaking into Mark Anderson's office and putting porn on the computer.

"Why did you do that?" asked Tim.

"I hate that asshole principal."

"And what are you going to do about it?" Peter challenged.

Daniel turned toward the mirror and pretended to adjust his tie. Tim grabbed Peter by the scruff of the neck and yanked him out of the chair.

"I'm sending you to family court and recommend the Youth Detention Center." Tim dropped him back in the chair.

"Hey, you can't do that to me, that's assault. He's a witness," he gestured to Daniel.

"Witness what?" asked Daniel. "I didn't see anything."

Murder in the Choir Room

"Assholes!" said Peter.

Peter was released to his parents, and I left the police station to head home. It was only four in the afternoon, and it was already getting dark. As I rounded the corner I saw a figure all bundled up on the street corner. Maybe I've spent too much time in cities, but something told me he was waiting for me. I was on full alert as he stepped into my path.

"Have you found Jesus?" he asked.

"Excuse me?" I said. Had I heard correctly?

"Have you found Jesus?" he asked again.

"I didn't know he was missing," I answered. "How very careless of you to have mislaid him!" I walked on as he glared after me. Everybody has the right to their own spiritual beliefs, and just as with unsolicited opinions, they should keep it to themselves.

I was annoyed and somewhat unnerved by the confrontation. I hurried home in the dark, but I kept turning around to check behind me. It felt like I was being followed, but I chalked it up to an over active imagination.

As it turned out, it wasn't my imagination it at all.

Stephen E. Stanley

Chapter 27

It was the Sunday before Christmas. Back in New Hampshire Rhonda and I shared the holidays with our small circle of friends. I would have a Christmas party at my place and Rhonda would host the New Year celebrations. Now here in Maine our circle of friends was bigger and more diverse than ever.

This year, in the spirit of diversity and sensitivity, I was calling it the "winter solstice celebration." Everyone was invited to bring a favorite dish. I was preparing a vegetable lasagna and several vegetable entrees. The house was decorated with white candles and evergreens. I built a small fire in the parlor stove, but I'd have to keep it small to keep the house from being overheated when it was full of people.

Jessica Mallory appeared. She had offered to help me set up. Tim was working and wouldn't show up until later. Jessica set up the buffet on the soapstone kitchen counter and I preheated the ovens for the casseroles that would be arriving. I put Jessica in charge of Argus so we could keep track of him in the crowd.

The first to arrive were my neighbors John and Dorothy Lowell followed by Beth White. Clearly Dorothy Lowell had been baking all afternoon. Beth had brought a large pot of mulled cider. I put it on the top of the parlor stove to keep warm. It filled the house with a sweet, spicy smell.

Jason and Monica came in the back door. Monica

put a pot of baked beans in the oven to warm up. Jason placed an ice-filled cooler full of beer on the kitchen floor. Argus ran into the kitchen and began sniffing the ice chest. Jessica came in and scooped him up, took Jason and Monica's jackets, and returned to the living room.

"Where's Tim?" asked Monica.

"He's working. He should be here in about an hour." Just then Billy Simpson walked in with several bottles of wine. All conversation stopped as we looked at him.

"Don't get your knickers in a twist," he said. "I found these shopping in Portland. They are non-alcoholic wines."

We all recovered quickly and gave him a group hug.

"I bet you did this for the shock value," said Monica.

"It worked, didn't it?" he replied. I left Monica in charge of the kitchen and went into the living room to greet the guests as they arrived.

"Bright blessings!" exclaimed Viola as she made her entrance through the front door. She had a large arrangement of flowers and a tray of crescent moon-shaped oat cakes. I placed the flowers on the coffee table. She was wearing a colorful patchwork dress with gold jewelry in place of her usual silver baubles.

"It feels like snow out there," she said.

"I haven't listened to the weather at all today." I replied.

"They said possible snow after sunset. But they never are right."

Stephen E. Stanley

"They say they can tell the weather," said Billy from behind me, "But they can't." Everyone agreed and the conversation turned into stories of how the weather forecasters had been wrong in predicating major storms.

Brian Stillwater arrived at the same time as Mary Bailey and her husband Clark. Mary brought a couscous salad, and Brian had a Native America dish made of corn and beans. More food arrived with Jackson Bennett and Rhonda. She was wearing a 1930's party dress and had a vintage hat that matched. Jackson, by contrast, was in jeans and a sweater. I rarely saw him out of a suit.

Mark Anderson and his wife Maggie came up the walkway as I opened the door. I wasn't sure Mark would show up after the recent problems, but since he was cleared of the charges, he took this as an opportunity to return to a normal life.

The sun was setting and the food was warming in the oven. Tim and Harry Kahill were the last to arrive. Harry had come from the hospital and Tim from the station. Tim hugged and kissed me. It wasn't like him to give public displays of affection.

"Christmas spirit get to you?" I asked.

"Big time," he said and hugged me again.

All the guests had broken into little groups. The two clergy women were off in the corner swapping horror stories about their congregations, I was pretty sure. The men were talking sports, and the women were either talking about their children or their careers. I really couldn't tell. Everyone had a drink. Some had beer, some had wine, some had hot cider and some just coffee.

Argus had gone around sniffing at everybody's feet. Jessica and I slipped into the kitchen to get the food ready. Argus followed us. He needed no encouragement. Wherever food is, that's where you'll find a pug. We placed the food on the counter and deserts on the table. There was no ham or turkey. It was agreed that, since some of the guests were vegetarian or semi-vegetarians, no meat would be served. I looked at the array of food. No one would miss meat with such a variety.

Back in the living room, I picked up the antique Shinto temple bell I had as a decoration and rang it. Everyone stopped talking and looked at me.

"Dinner is ready," I announced. "Because this is the celebration of the Winter Solstice, I've asked our resident Pagan, Viola, to offer the blessing."

"Please gather around and make a circle," requested Viola. Without being instructed to do so, everyone held hands as we gathered in a circle. I was surprised at how many people I could fit in my small house.

"May the spirits of love and friendship bless this gathering. May the food we enjoy bless our lives and enrich our bodies. Let us be keepers of peace and servants of the poor, knowing that we are one with the earth," prayed Viola.

"Okay, everyone, the food is in the kitchen. Grab a plate and enjoy. There is more than enough food." No one wanted to be the first in line, but gradually everyone drifted into the kitchen, filled up their plates, and drifted back into the living room and sat in small groups. I gave Argus a new nylon chew toy, which he ran into the living room with and started to chew. I put on some soft, New Age music in the background and headed for the kitchen. Tim, Jessica, and I were the last to serve ourselves. There was plenty of food left.

"Good turn out," observed Tim as he joined me sitting on the floor in the corner.

"Everyone I invited showed up."

"Sorry I couldn't be here to help set up."

"Jessica was here. She was a great help."

"You better believe it," said Jessica as she sat down with us.

"But I could never get her to clean her room," teased Tim.

"Sucks to be a parent," replied Jessica. "Just ask my mother."

"No thanks," said Tim. "The less I have to speak to that woman, the better."

"You should have seen her face when I told her about you and Jesse. She was livid! It was wonderful!"

The utility cart I had put out was getting filled up with dirty dishes. People had gone back for seconds and were now well into the desert and coffee. The level of conversation had increased as people had progressed through the meal.

I went into the kitchen to refill my glass with more

wine when I heard a thud followed by a scream. Looking through the kitchen pass-through I saw Harry Kahill kneeling over John Lowell.

"Call nine-one-one," he said. Tim already had the phone in his hand and was speaking to the dispatcher.

"What happened?" I asked Rhonda, who was standing by the kitchen door.

"John Lowell was talking and suddenly collapsed."

"Thank God there was a doctor here." I observed. It was only a matter of a few minutes until the ambulance pulled up. Harry and Dorothy rode with John in the ambulance. Tim followed in his police car. The rest of us returned to a more somber celebration. We knew there was nothing we could do, but no one was going home until we had some word from the hospital. Jessica had made herself useful by going in the kitchen and washing out the casserole dishes to be returned to their owners.

"Thanks Jessica for helping out."

"No problem, step-dad," she replied.

"Step-dad?"

"Get used to it, Jesse, you're in my father's family now!" she laughed.

"Attention everyone!" yelled Rhonda in an effort to lighten the mood. "I have an announcement. Everyone is invited to my house for New Year's Eve. But you have to come in costume." There followed a series of muffled comments. I wasn't sure the costume thing would work out.

Stephen E. Stanley

"And the big news is that Jackson and I just bought a house together. We closed on it two weeks ago, so it will be up and running by New Year's Eve." That set off another round of muffled comments.

"There's more," she added. With Rhonda there was always more. "We bought Dr. Monroe's old house." Dr. Monroe had been a fixture in Bath for the last sixty years. His house was a large Queen Anne Victorian on the river just north of downtown. Everyone knew where it was.

As soon as I could, I took her aside. "When did all this happen?" I asked. "And why haven't you said anything before now?"

"Jackson and I have been working on it for a while now. We were keeping it a secret as a surprise later on, but now seemed as good a time as any for a surprise."

"It certainly is a surprise!" I said somewhat irritated that I wasn't in on the secret.

"It was a compromise. Jackson wanted to get married and I didn't, so this is what we worked out."

"Well I…" I began but the phone rang and I jumped up to grab it. It was Tim. I listened carefully and hung up. Everyone was looking at me.

"As near as they can tell, John Lowell passed out from low blood pressure. They are going to keep him in the hospital overnight just as a precaution. But once they adjust his blood pressure medicine, he should be fine." People began to talk again in their normal voices, no more hushed tones. I knew the party was breaking up soon, so I circulated the room with a plateful of chocolates and other candies. If they didn't eat it, then I probably would, and me on a sugar high is not pretty!

Mark and his wife were the first to leave and, as usually happens, people started leaving in short order. Soon it was only Rhonda and Jackson, Jessica, and me. We were waiting for Tim to return.

Argus was the first to hear Tim drive up. Tim entered covered with snow.

"Snowing hard?" asked Jessica.

"It's just beginning, but yes it is," he said. "What did I miss."

"Just the announcement of the century." I went on and told him about Rhonda and Jackson's purchase.

"You've only got two weeks to get it in shape for New Years," Tim pointed out.

"We've already had the painters in and have new furniture coming. We'll be ready."

"What about your condo?" I asked.

"It's already on the market."

"Sounds like you've got all the bases covered," Tim said.

"Let's hope so," said Jackson.

Chapter 28

The smell of coffee woke me up early. Jessica had spent the night in the guest room because it was too late to drive home, and she offered to help clean up in the morning.

"Young people never get up before noon," I observed as I walked into the kitchen where Jessica was working. Argus was running ahead of me, looking for a treat.

"Stereotyping? I'm surprised at you. And for your information, I take morning classes at the university. By the way, I found one of your recipes for breakfast casserole, and it's in the oven. I've heard how you hate to make breakfast."

"You've heard correctly. You're a good kid Jessica, if I haven't said it before."

"You have, but feel free to keep saying it, step-dad."

"What's going on?" asked Tim as he stumbled into the kitchen. Jessica poured us all some coffee.

"Nothing much," I answered. "It feels like the middle of the night. It's so dark out."

"Maybe if you opened the shades, it might help." Tim went into the living room and pulled up the shades. "Never mind, It didn't help."

"Told you it was dark."

"Did all the guests leave last night?" asked Tim.

"I think so. I didn't see anyone passed out in the corner. Why?"

"There's a black Honda parked across the street that I don't recognize."

I went to the window to look out at the street. The

Honda was parked in the shadows of a tree. It's a small, dead end street, so we aren't use to unfamiliar cars. Just then the Honda pulled out of the shadows and flew down the street without lights.

"That's odd," observed Tim.

"Maybe it was just someone who was lost and checking the GPS."

"Breakfast is ready!" called Jessica from the kitchen.

"Smells great!" I said as I sat down.

"Tastes great!" added Tim as he tasted it.

"You'll make some guy a great wife," I said to her. She picked up a spoon and threw it at me. I ducked and it went clattering to the floor.

"Just remember my father's favorite saying, 'Don't be an asshole!'" she added.

"John Lowell should be home today. It was just a one night observation," Tim said to change the subject.

The overnight observation reminded me of something. "Tim, when they kept you overnight, they took a blood sample to see if you ingested anything, didn't they?"

"Yes, they did," he answered.

"Did they find anything?"

"Not as far as I know. Harry Kahill had the lab results sent to him. He said he'd let me know if they found anything. But if I didn't hear, then it meant that nothing was found."

"It pays to be friends with a doctor, I guess." I

observed.

"Not to mention the chief of police." added Tim.

"There are some benefits to that, indeed," I replied. Jessica just rolled her eyes.

After my second cup of coffee, I was able to focus a little more. I noticed that Jessica had already done one load of dishes.

"Thanks for helping clean up," I said to her.

"Why don't you go off to Erebus, and I'll finish cleaning up. Argus can stay with me for the day."

"I need to run home and change and go in to work," said Tim as he flew out of the house.

"He works too hard," I said to Jessica when he had left the house.

"Nothing new about that," she replied.

I was once again surprised to find Viola in the shop before Rhonda.

"Rhonda asked me to open," said Viola before I could ask. "She's working on her house." Today she was dressed in a full length black dress, white blouse, and a colorfully embroidered vest.

"Great. I'll go put the coffee on." I said as I headed to the back room. There were a ton of orders to fill, and I would have to ship them overnight for them to make it to their destination for Christmas. I checked my personal email and I had a note from my old friend Alex Tate suggesting we get together for lunch after New Years. I looked at my calendar and suggested several dates. I had another email from Parker Reed, an old friend from Camden, who was planning to crew on a windjammer off the Florida coast after the new year. Parker had been friends with Billy Simpson off and on for the past year and wanted my thoughts on Billy's recovery. I wrote that I thought it was going well and that Billy might appreciate a call from Parker.

At noon Tim stopped by with two Italian sandwiches and a big bag of chips. The Jack Riley case was growing colder by the hour.

"Any new leads?" I asked.

"Irene Bancroft was in Lake Placid when he was killed. So she is in the clear for murder, though she'll be tried for embezzlement. His business partner, Kathy Bowen, has an alibi. Mark Anderson has been cleared, so far. But there are still lots of people who hated Jack."

"I just think we are missing something. I feel like the person is right in front of our noses."

"You always say that," Tim reminded me.

"I know, but..." I stopped in mid sentence as a horrible image flashed through my mind. "Tim, who was the actual last person to see Jack Riley?"

"The killer, of course."

"I mean, as far as we know?"

"Billy Simpson," answered Tim. "But you don't suspect him do you? As far as I know he didn't even know Jack Riley very well."

"I think we need to look at everything. Remember

Billy disappeared after the murder. And he didn't tell any of us where he was. He just dropped out of sight. And what happened to him? What was the last straw that sent him off to rehab?" I asked. The images in my mind were coming at me fast. So fast I was only able to focus on one or two. But those one or two images all said the same thing to me.

"Tim, we've been focusing on just Jack Riley. We know he made business trips to various places like Lake Placid and New York City, supposedly on business. But have you ever asked if there was anyone else with him?"

"No, not directly," answered Tim.

"Send out some pictures of Jack and Billy and see if anyone remembers seeing them together."

Tim looked at me like I had lost my mind. "Are you serious?" he asked.

"I'm just telling you what the voices in my head are saying," I replied. Tim rolled his eyes heavenward and sighed.

At three o'clock Brad Watkins came into Erebus and Viola ended her shift. I was still catching up on orders. I expected next year to be busier, and if so, we might have to hire more people.

"Hey Jesse, I see you're still working," said Brad as he came into the backroom to hang up his coat.

"Almost caught up," I replied. "These orders can go out tonight when the UPS truck rolls up."

"Okay, I'll keep a watch out for him. Did you see

that guy passing out Jesus literature out front?"

"No. It's probably the same guy I ran into yesterday. He was kind of creepy looking."

"That's him there," said Brad pointing out the back window toward the parking lot. I looked; it was the same guy. He was putting pamphlets on car windshields.

"Should we call the police?" asked Brad.

"No," I answered. "He's exercising his right to free speech. Nothing illegal about that."

"Too bad! Well, I should get out front," said Brad and left for the main counter.

I reached for the phone and punched in Monica's number. She picked up after the third ring. I figured she checked the caller ID first.

"Am I going crazy?" I asked.

"Yes!" she replied before I could elaborate in greater detail.

"You didn't let me finish," I replied. I told her about the flashing images in my mind when the subject of Billy Simpson and Jack Riley came up.

"You need to trust your gut. Those images flashing through your head are coming from your subconscious. Somewhere in your head, your subconscious is fitting some pieces together. Those images will come together soon, and then you'll see them clearly."

"Thanks," I said. I needed to hear it.

"When will you learn to trust that voice inside your head?"

"Give me another fifty years and I might get there."

"But to answer your earlier question, yes you are crazy!"

"This is the sound of me hanging up now," I said as I hit the off button.

It was dark by the time I passed the last package over to the UPS driver. I said good night to Brad and headed out the back to the parking lot. It was dark in the lot and I thought one of the street lights must have burned out. I heard someone behind me as I got near my car. I started to turn around and slipped. I felt something hit my head. I felt a pain, saw some lights, and then everything went black.

Chapter 29

Cold and confusion were all I could grasp as I tried to focus my eyes. I heard voices, but I couldn't seem to understand what they were saying.

"Jesse, can you hear me?" The voice seemed familiar.

"My head hurts," I replied. My eyes began to focus, and I saw Brad Watkins and a very concerned looking Tim Mallory. They tried to lift me off the ground, and it took them a few tries before I could stand upright. Maybe it was their way of suggesting that it was time for a diet. There was a police cruiser with blue lights flashing nearby. Tim and Brad walked me over to the car and put me in the backseat. The car was nice and warm.

"We're going to the emergency room," said Tim as he got behind the wheel.

"I'm fine," I tried to protest, but it came out all slurred. Everything looked surreal as I looked out of the window into the black evening outside. I seemed to drift in and out of reality because the next thing I realized I was sitting on an examining table under bright lights.

"Mild concussion," said the doctor as she checked the reaction of my pupils to a flashlight. "Just watch him for a day or two. Give him some aspirin for the pain as needed." Somehow I got home and in bed, but my memory of the night is still pretty sketchy.

It was Christmas Eve day, and my head still hurt. Jessica had volunteered to deliver my gift baskets so I could take it easy. I was determined to sing in the choir for the Christmas Eve service, but I knew I had to rest up if I had any chance of making it to the evening rehearsal.

I was propped up on pillows on my bed reading with Argus curled up on my feet keeping them warm. I really had no memory of the fall. I didn't know if I had slipped on the ice, been hit on the head by an attacker, or been pushed by someone in the back alley. Brad had looked out the back window and seen me on the ground, but he hadn't seen me fall. He called Tim and then rushed out to see if I was okay. The police station was only a block away. Tim had run the distance and called for backup.

The police had scoured the area, but found no one. The guy putting religious leaflets on the cars was nowhere to be found. Tim wanted to find him. I just wanted to forget the whole thing.

I was well into my book when Argus leaped off the bed and ran toward the door as Tim arrived. Nobody can sneak into a house with an alert dog.

"Here," said Tim as he passed me a pen and a pad of notepaper.

"What's this?" I asked.

"I want you to write down tonight's winning lottery numbers!"

"What are you talking about?"

"You were right about Billy Simpson. I sent a photo to the Lake Placid police. They showed Jack and Billy's photos around. The motel manager and a diner waitress both recognized them. They were there together."

"Wow!" I said. I had even impressed myself this time.

"I think he has to go on the suspect list."

"Just because they knew each other and traveled together?"

"You think traveling was all they were doing?" asked Tim.

"No, I guess not. But with Jack Riley? Yuk!"

"It's worth looking at," said Tim. "I need to get back to work and let you rest up for tonight." Argus ran with Tim to the door, and then ran back to the bedroom, jumped on the bed and curled back up on my feet.

It wasn't going to be a white Christmas this year. There had been a few snow showers, but the snow had melted each time. Despite the images on Christmas cards, a white Christmas in Maine was not guaranteed.

The church ladies had spent the day decorating the church for Christmas. The purple Advent sanctuary colors had been exchanged for festive white. Every window had candles, and evergreens were abundant. A Christmas tree decorated with mittens, gloves, and hats stood in the corner. They would be distributed to the poor and homeless tomorrow. The smell of evergreens and beeswax filled the air.

Rob Sinclair was playing the organ and trying to

conduct the choir at the same time. We were trying to sing "In the Deep Midwinter," by the Victorian poet Christina Rossetti and music by Gustav Holst. By the third try we were able to make it all the way through without sounding like a herd of sheep. Rob motioned us back to the choir room as the church began to fill up with people. Christmas and Easter are the busiest times for a church. Even people who normally shun Sunday services in favor of shopping or recreation seem to feel a need for spiritual acknowledgment at these seasonal celebrations.

At seven o'clock the choir had gathered in the back of the darkened church. We watched as the deacons lit the candles one by one. The organ started the processional hymn "O Come All Ye Faithful!" and we in the choir headed to the choir stalls. The overflow crowd was seated in the balcony. I was impressed with the turnout. Maybe it was the candlelight and the music, but I was feeling very optimistic about the future. If we could all come together as a community for one hour of shared peace, maybe there was hope for humanity.

By the time we stood up in the choir to sing the anthem, our voices had warmed up and we sounded, if not great, at least confident. After the service it took quite a while for the church to empty out. I think people wanted to savor the experience for a while longer. Tim and Jessica waited for me at the door. Monica and Jason were joining us at Eagle's Nest for a late Christmas Eve supper of seafood chowder and biscuits.

Murder in the Choir Room

*****

The Christmas gifts were wrapped up and packed into the car. Tim and I were on our way to Christmas dinner. I drove and Tim lay back in the passenger seat with his eyes closed. I could tell he was tired by the deeply etched lines in his face. I pulled the car into a parking space at the Sagadahoc Nursing Home. We were having Christmas dinner with Old Lady Lafond.

"Don't you have something better to do on Christmas Day?" asked Mrs. Lafond as we entered her room.

"Not at all!" answered Tim as we each gave her a kiss on the cheek. She looked pleased to see us, or at least pleased to see Tim. I still had the suspicion that she considered me the slow one in the class. She carefully unwrapped the gift we brought her.

"This looks very old," she said when she saw the antique paper weight.

"Tim thought you might use it to throw at a nurse when you have one of your spells," I said.

"I don't have spells!"

"Yes, you do!" I answered.

"Name one!" she challenged.

"June 3, 1970. Last period study hall. You threw a chalk eraser at my head!"

"You were passing notes and flirting with Elaine Goldstein as usual."

"So what?" I asked.

"I just thought she could do better!"

"You're a hateful old woman!" I muttered.

"I try my best," she answered and smiled.

A nurse came by and told us it was dinner time. We each took an arm and walked Beatrice to the dining room. Though she was feisty, she felt frail. The dining room had decorations up and a tree in the corner trying to make the place less institutional and more homelike. It was a failure. Many of the residents had guests with them today, but some didn't. I noticed the nurses making sure that those with no family received extra attention.

"Have you solved the Jack Riley murder yet?" Beatrice asked Tim.

"Not yet. There are just too many dead ends in this case."

"I'll bet you find that this is even bigger than murder."

"You may be right," replied Tim.

"Is it possible that there might be more than one person involved? You said that lots of people hated him."

"It could be," said Tim. "But I don't have any physical evidence linking anyone yet."

"Well, I'm confident that you can solve this, Timothy," and she turned to me, "And maybe this one can help."

"I hope you're right, on both counts!" replied Tim unnecessarily.

"My experience," she continued, "is that there is

someone right under your nose, who is very quiet and just sort of fades into the background. Someone you never suspect. Just like kids in a classroom. Sometimes the biggest trouble makers are the quiet kids working below the radar."

"You've got that right!" I agreed as I tried to avoid the radar beams.

The food arrived. There were strained vegetables and turkey cut up into small bites.

"Some of us still have our own teeth you know!" said Beatrice to the server. The server just smiled. "She was one of my students and now she feeds me my dinner."

"There's something to think about," I replied.

"So, Tim," began Beatrice. "What are you planning to do when you retire. You've never been able to sit still."

"Jesse thinks I should be a private investigator. What do you think?"

"I think you'd make a good one. But you need to get this guy to help," she pointed at me. "You'll do well in the field, but you need someone to organize."

"Me?" I said.

"Sure," she replied. "What are you doing now? Writing out recipes and working in the back of a store. You need to get a life!"

I hadn't looked at it quite that way. Maybe I was getting too settled.

Stephen E. Stanley

Billy Simpson sat on my sofa on the day after Christmas and was being questioned by Tim. Tim thought it would be easier to question him in an informal setting. Police examination rooms do nothing to put people at ease.

"I've told you everything I know," protested Billy.

"Then why did you lie about Jack Riley?" asked Tim in his police voice.

"I didn't lie. I just neglected to tell you that I went away with Jack for a few days."

"Why," I asked.

"I didn't think that it had any bearing on the murder."

"Everything," said Tim, "has a bearing on the murder."

"Did anyone else know that you were..." I looked for the right word, "Seeing Jack Riley?"

"I never told anyone. But Jack said he was going to tell his wife if she started to nag him again. He said she was a bitch, and he wanted to give her something to think about."

"Do you think he told her?" I asked.

"I don't know," he answered. "Can I go now?"

Tim nodded his head. "Don't leave town." I didn't think he was joking.

"See you guys," waved Billy on his way out. "Thanks for not making me go to the station, Tim."

"No problem," replied Tim. When Billy was gone Tim turned to me. "I guess we have to take a closer look at the wife. This case just goes around in circles and doesn't go anywhere."

"Time to take a break, big guy," I said.

"Any ideas on what to do now? We seem to be alone."

"Just one," I said. "Follow me!"

Erebus was extremely busy between Christmas and New Year's Day. People were retuning or exchanging items both in the store and online. Argus and I had a busy day ahead of us at the shop. Viola was left in charge of the front while I worked on the mail orders. Occasionally I had to help her when she had a crowded store. Rhonda was still trying to get her new house ready for her New Year's Eve party. Good luck with that! I suspected I'd be called in to help with her decorating ideas in the next few days.

I was meeting Tim for lunch at Maxwell's. He had asked Molly Riley for lunch to interview her.

"Why don't you just call her down to the police station? " I had asked earlier.

"People are more at ease out in public. And the truth is I'm trying to get a feel for private investigation. I won't have a police station after I retire."

"Good point," I agreed.

"You think Old Lady Lafond is right?" I asked. "That there is someone right in the middle of this that we are not seeing?"

"It's possible," Tim sighed. "But I've been racking my brain and I can't imagine who it is." Tim was dressed in a white shirt and red tie. If he smiled with those perfect white teeth, Molly Riley would have no chance. She'd tell all. At least I knew it worked on me.

We had ordered coffee when Molly Riley was led to our table. She was a petite middle-aged woman with light brown hair that hung loose around her shoulders. She immediately greeted Tim.

"It's good to see you, chief Mallory. Oh, hi, Jesse," she said. Just as I suspected, next to Tim I was invisible.

"Good to see you too, Molly," replied Tim. I just gave her a wave. We ordered lunch and exchanged small talk through the meal. Once the dishes were cleared away and the server refilled our coffee, we got down to business.

"I need you to tell me as much as you know about your husband, his business, and his trips. However trivial or unrelated you think it is, you need to level with us. At this point almost anything could be a clue."

Molly looked at me. "I'm just here for moral support," I said. She nodded.

"Let's start with Jack. Did he seem upset or agitated in the last few days before he was killed?"

"No, everything seemed to be normal."

"Any unusual phone calls at home? Any visitors?" I asked.

"Nothing like that. He did work late on Thursday and Friday evenings, but that wasn't so unusual."

"Had he always worked late or was this a new development?" asked Tim.

Murder in the Choir Room

Molly thought about it before she spoke. "He started working late one or two nights a week at the beginning of summer. Before that he never worked late."

"You said that you thought his business partner had something to do with it. Do you think they were having an affair?" I asked.

Molly laughed. "Jack hated her guts. He wouldn't be having an affair with her! She wasn't his type."

"Was he having an affair with someone, do you think?" Tim asked.

"I don't see what this has to do with Jack's death," she answered.

"I need answers," said Tim. "Almost anything I find out could be useful."

Molly sat up straight and glared at Tim. Tim sat there expressionless and waited. Finally Molly slumped back in her chair and looked deflated. "I'll be the laughing stock of the town if this gets out."

"Tell us," Tim said quietly.

"He told me he was seeing someone. He didn't say who, but he said he was going to enjoy what he could."

"If he was cheating on you with another woman, that would hardly make you a laughing stock," I replied.

"He was seeing a man!" she almost shouted.
"I couldn't believe it. I felt like an idiot."

"You weren't the idiot," I said to her as I covered her hand with mine. Billy Simpson was the idiot, I thought to myself.

"Do you know who it was or did you suspect someone?" asked Tim.

"No, I don't," she answered. "I don't care anymore."

"What can you tell us about his trips?" asked Tim to change the subject.

"As far as I know, they all had to do with sending American doctors to poor sections of South America. He did some recruiting and helped with fund raising."

"How long was he involved with this organization?" I asked.

"Only about a year. It was all new to him, but he seemed to enjoy it."

"How often did he go away?" Tim asked.

"He took about five trips during the past year. Most of the trips were to the headquarters at Lake Placid, but two of the trips were to San Francisco."

"Did he go alone?" I asked.

"No, he always traveled with a group. They went together."

"Can you get us a list of their names?" Tim asked.

"I'll try," she answered. We spent some more time asking how her kids were doing. They seemed to be doing well and were supportive of their mother. Molly thanked us for lunch and excused herself.

"What do you think?" asked Tim.

"I think she knows more than she is telling us. I know it must be embarrassing for her, but I'm not sure we can get her to say anymore. Still, I can't get the disturbing images of Billy Simpson and Jack Riley doing the nasty out of my head," I answered.

Tim just shook his head. "What the hell was Billy thinking?"

Chapter 30

The end of December in Maine was the coldest since 1978. That year the temperature dropped to twenty-five degrees below zero. This year it wasn't quite that cold, but the night time temperature was minus ten degrees and by noon of December thirty-first it had warmed up to a tropical minus four.

I wanted nothing more than to stay home by a roaring fire and try to stay warm. However it was the night of Rhonda's New Year's Eve party, and I had to go and be a good friend. Earlier in the day I made a red velvet cake to take to the party. It was always good for a conversation starter. The white frosted outside looks pedestrian enough, but once cut, it reveals a bright red cake interior. The origin of the cake is one of the more fascinating urban legends. According to the story a woman visited the Waldorf Astoria's dining room in New York sometime in the 1930's. She was so impressed with the red velvet cake desert that she wrote to the hotel for the recipe. She received the recipe, along with a bill for thirty dollars, a shocking amount of money for the times. Her lawyer told her that she had no option but to pay the bill. To get even she distributed the recipe for free to everyone she knew. Of course the story is not true, but it sounds believable to party guests after they've belted back a few jello shots.

I was anxious to see Rhonda's new house. She hadn't asked me for any help, which was surprising. Maybe she had hired a professional decorator, after all Jackson

Bennett was well-off, even if Rhonda wasn't. I was, at the moment, trying to decorate myself for the costume party.

Tim had the good luck to borrow a fire fighter's uniform from one of his buddies at the fire station. I was dressing up as a utility worker. I had on a navy jumpsuit with my name embroidered on the pocket. I added a tool belt and a hard hat. I actually looked pretty convincing, which could either be good or bad, depending on how you looked at it.

I had the car warming up as we put the finishing touches on our costumes. No way was I getting in a cold car for the mile ride to Rhonda's house.

"You about ready?" asked Tim.

"Ready!" I said as I put the cake in a cake carrier. "Let's go!"

The ride through town was quiet. It was too cold for anyone to be out. We pulled on to Bowery Street and parked near Rhonda's house. The house was ablaze with light. The big wrap-around porch had buckets of beer and wine cooling outside. No need of ice tonight. I rang the bell and Rhonda came to the door. I looked at her in horror!

"Completely and utterly tasteless," I said to her. She was dressed as Jackie Kennedy in the famous pink suite and pillbox hat, complete with bloodstains!

"Too soon?" she asked.

"Too late," I replied as we stepped through the door and passed her the cake. "Probably most of the people here weren't even born when Kennedy was assassinated."

"Hey, Jackson," greeted Tim. Jackson was dressed

as a pirate. I was relieved. I half expected him to be dressed as JFK, complete with exploded head. I looked around at the various costumes. Viola was dressed as a witch; big surprise there! Monica and Jason were dressed as Pilgrims, Mary Bailey was dressed as the pope, and Billy Simpson was dressed as a sailor. With Billy was someone in a sea captain's uniform. He had his back to me so I couldn't see him. There were lots of people I didn't recognize; I figured they must be friends and business associates of Jackson.

"Shit!" I said out loud when the sea captain turned around and waved at me.

"Who is that?" asked Tim as he checked out the sea captain.

"That," I said, "is Parker Reed." Parker Reed and I met years ago when he was the first mate on a windjammer cruise out of Camden. I was the substitute cook when the real cook decided to jump ship in mid voyage. I spent the rest of the summer cooking on the ship, and Parker Reed and I were an item. Parker was ten years younger than me and he was very good looking. He also liked older men and now was the on-again off-again boy toy for Billy Simpson. Apparently it was on-again. It was my lifelong ambition to keep Tim Mallory and Parker Reed from ever meeting.

Parker Reed came over and gave me a hug. He put out his hand to Tim. "Parker Reed" They shook hands. I though Parker kept his hand in Tim's a little too long. It was clear that Parker was checking out Tim and liked what he saw. I could tell that Parker had already had a few and might become a handful.

"Wow!" said Parker, "A fireman. I bet you've got a big hose!"

"I think Billy is looking for you," I said to Parker. I waved Billy over to our group.

"I forgot you two hadn't met," said Billy indicating Parker and Tim. "Where's Jessica tonight?" Billy seemed oblivious to the fact that Parker was flirting with all the men.

"Jessica is having her own party at my house. She wanted to be with people her own age, and I like the idea of knowing where she is," answered Tim.

"Jesse and Tim," said our hostess as she stepped up to our little group. "Let me give you the tour."

Rhonda led us around the house. The place was classically decorated in late Victorian cottage style. The huge living room had large windows that looked out on the river. The kitchen was modern with granite and stainless steel, but lots of original detail and built-ins as well. Off the kitchen was a screen porch that faced the sloping backyard and the river beyond. The dining room had an original marble mantel topped with a huge mirror. Over the dining table was a beautiful electrified gas chandelier. The front hall had a sweeping staircase and the bedrooms upstairs were large, but not nearly as ornate as the public rooms.

"This was built as a summer cottage in 1878," explained Jackson as he joined us on the tour.

"Rhonda, this is beautiful," said Tim who is not easily moved by architecture.

Stephen E. Stanley

"And so unlike you!" I added. Rhonda had always been sparse and utilitarian in her housing choices. She flipped me the bird.

"It's Jackson," she explained. "He went to the furniture store, asked to speak to the decorator, and together they went through the house and picked out the pieces. The only thing I did was clean and paint."

"You painted?" I asked.

"Well, I hired the painters," she admitted.

We joined the rest of the guests in the huge living room. I always manage to find the most boring person in the room, and then end up listening to a story that seems to have no end. I tried to signal to Tim to come and rescue me, but he, too, seemed to be stuck in the conversation black hole. I was finally able to break away and went into the kitchen to help Rhonda put out the food. I was bent over the counter taking the cake out of the cake keeper when I felt two hands on my ass. For some reason I didn't think it was Tim. I turned around.

"Parker, what are you doing?" I knew exactly what he was doing, but thought it wise to play dumb.

"Checking out the merchandise. Still firm and ripe for picking. Want to spend a few minutes in the pantry?" he asked.

As memories came flooding back it was tempting. "Don't you remember the old saying? 'You dance with the one who brought you!'"

"And here's another saying: 'Life is short!'"

"Which one of you should I shoot first?" asked Tim standing in the kitchen door. He wasn't smiling.

"Him!" I said pointing to Parker. Tim came over and stood beside me. Parker looked Tim up and down. Parker sighed and left the kitchen.

"This is the guy you worked with on the windjammer?" Tim asked.

"Well, there might have been a little more to it than that," I admitted.

"And you guys shared a cabin?"

"Yes, we shared a crew cabin," I answered.

"I'm guessing there might have been nudity involved to some degree?" Clearly Tim was enjoying watching me squirm.

"Maybe."

"I'll bet Billy has his hands full," observed Tim.

"I'd put money on it."

It was getting close to midnight and the temperature was dropping. The house was nice and warm because it was filled with people, but anytime I walked by a window I could feel the cold radiating from the glass. Harry Kahill walked up to me eating a piece of cake.

"How's your head?" he asked.

"It's much better. How did you hear about that?" I asked. He wasn't on duty the night I showed up in the emergency room.

"Hospital gossip. Watch out for signs of brain injury. Sometimes a concussion can bring about memory loss."

Stephen E. Stanley

"I already have memory loss," I said. "It's called getting old."

"I hear you!" laughed Harry.

"Attention everyone!" yelled Jackson. "Gather together. We're getting ready for the countdown" I looked around the room. Maybe it was the two glasses of wine that I drank, but looking around I realized how comic we all looked. A bunch of adults, mostly well into middle age, dressed up in weird costumes and gathered together to usher in midnight. People went to the table and grabbed party hats and noise makers and then made a circle in the room.

"Ten! Nine! Eight! Seven! Six! Five! Four! Three! Two! One! Happy New Year!" everyone shouted together. Noise makers went off and we saw the beginning of the New Year!

It was a cold ride home, and I was grateful to crawl into a warm bed. Argus buried himself under the top comforter and snuggled between me and Tim.

"What's with the dog?" asked Tim.

"He hates cold weather, and it's a good excuse for him to sleep under the comforter.

"Happy New Year, by the way," said a sleepy Tim.

"It will be, if I have anything to do with it," I replied.

The temperature the next morning was eight below zero. I built a fire and we had our morning coffee in the living room.

Murder in the Choir Room

"So what is your New Year's resolution?" I asked Tim

"To retire and to find Jack Riley's killer."

"What's yours?" he asked.

"To enjoy life to the fullest!"

"Good Plan!"

"So where are we with the Riley case?" I asked. Tim raised his eyebrows at the "we" part of the question, but didn't say anything.

"Right now there are only two suspects, and they are both very shaky: Molly Riley and Billy Simpson. But their motives are weak and there is no evidence linking them."

"But they were both in church!" I said.

"That's the problem. Everyone was in church. The killer was probably in church. But anybody could have slipped out of the pews and not been noticed. Everyone was involved in the service, not keeping track of who was or was not there."

"So, unless there is a break in the case with some new evidence. The murder will go unsolved."

"That's pretty much it!" answered Tim. "I need to go home and change for work. And I have to appraise the damage from Jessica's party."

"Jackson, Billy, and Jason are coming over for the football game. We'll be here when you get off work. And plan to stay late!"

Stephen E. Stanley

Chapter 31

The Canadian cold front that had enveloped New England and brought the sub-zero weather had receded and warmer air had taken its place. We were experiencing the January thaw. The daytime temperatures in early January reached the mid forties during the day and dipped just below freezing at night. The only problem was that nights seemed to be about twenty-five hours long. There was still no significant snow fall, though a low pressure system was coming toward us from the west and had already dumped a few feet in Colorado.

"I hear you guys had a great time watching footfall," said Rhonda as I hung up my coat and unharnessed Argus in the backroom of Erebus. Today she was dressed in a 1940s suite with padded shoulders. She bore an uncanny resemblance to Joan Crawford. I wanted to scream "No wire hangers!" but resisted the urge.

"Yes, we did. The Patriots weren't playing so we really didn't care who won, but the game was exciting."

"So that was Parker Reed!" Rhonda said, I knew she was digging for the whole story. "That was one hot sea captain!"

"I was afraid he might take a liking to Tim, but he seemed to behave himself after a while."

"He was clearly after you, though I don't think Billy noticed it. I brought in some leftover goodies from the party, so we can have lunch here. There is plenty."

"How's business?" I asked.

Murder in the Choir Room

"It's been slow, just like last January. Things will pick up. I thought today we would do inventory when Viola comes in."

"Okay." As if on cue Viola walked into the store.

"Bright Blessings everyone!" The bright blessing thing was getting old. Today she was dressed in something that looked like a flannel monk's robe.

"You both realize that the costume party is over, don't you?" I had to say it.

"Don't be an asshole!" was Rhonda's response.

"And don't mess with the witches," added Viola.

"How about if I go to the coffee shop and get us some lattes to celebrate the new year?" I offered.

They both thought that was a great idea. The truth was none of us was excited about doing inventory. The coffee shop was only a few doors down from Erebus.

"Good morning, Jesse," greeted Brian Stillwater behind the counter.

"Good morning Brian. How's everything?"

"Couldn't be better. What can I do for you?"

"Three lattes to go. One a decaf." The last thing I needed was for Rhonda to be on a caffeine high.

"No problem. It will take me just a few minutes to get the machine up and running."

"Take your time," I replied. I spotted Harry Kahill sitting in the corner.

"Good morning Harry. How are you doing?"

"That was some party at Rhonda's. I left right

around midnight."

"I don't think I saw you leave."

"I actually didn't have a real costume. I came in my scrubs and wore a mask. I only stayed an hour between shifts at the hospital. As you can imagine the emergency room is very busy on New Year's Eve."

"It was pretty much over at midnight."

"How's Tim doing on the Riley murder?" Harry asked.

"I think it's more or less a dead end at this point."

"I've been thinking about that day," Harry motioned me to sit down. " As you know I was on call and had to leave before the end of the service."

"Yes?" I didn't see where this was going.

"Well, that's just it. If someone leaves before the end of the service, the head usher usually opens the door for them and closes the door after them because it's less disruptive than having the door slam."

"I don't follow," I said.

"Billy Simpson was the head usher. He disappeared before the end of the service. In fact, I thought I saw him walking down the hallway toward the choir room. But I can't be sure."

"Have you told Tim any of this?" I asked.

"Do you think I should? Billy is a patient of mine, and I don't want to get him in trouble. Besides it's all circumstantial. I could be wrong."

"I think you should at least tell Tim. Let him decide

what to do with your observations."

Harry sighed and said he would go see Tim. Brian signaled that the lattes were ready and I picked them up and took them back to the shop. After the lattes we did the inventory. It was better than a root canal, but not much better!

The low pressure system that was sweeping across the country finally made it into Maine. The TV weather people had been nearly hysterical about a possible storm. Several inches of snow were predicted. Years of observation had taught me that weather people were prone to fantasy and wishful thinking. Still a majority of viewers headed to the stores to gather emergency supplies. I think it's a plot by the television stations to whip up storm frenzy. First of all, it increases their viewership. Second of all, some of their most important advertisers are the grocery chains. Sounds like a set-up to me.

I wasn't worried. I have a well-stocked pantry all year long. Bring it on! By five o'clock the rain started and it was raining hard. Where was the snow? Tim came in from work as I was getting dinner ready.

"It smells good in here. What's for dinner?"

"I made a big pan of lasagna. How's the weather?"

"It's getting colder. The rain may turn to snow or maybe ice."

"Snow would be okay; freezing rain is never good. What's wrong? You've got that look on your face."

"Harry Kahill came to see me today. I know he told you about what he saw."

"You mean what he *thinks* he saw. He doesn't seem too sure about it." I replied.

"Still, I think it's time to bring Billy in for official questioning."

"But you can't charge him with anything. You have no proof," I protested.

"I'll bring him in as a material witness."

"This sucks!" I said.

"I know, but it's my job."

I took the lasagna out of the oven and left it to cool while I prepared the broccoli. "Well, let's enjoy dinner, and maybe later I can get your mind off work."

"I can think of at least a dozen scenarios for that!"

The weather forecasters were wrong as usual. It continued to rain as the temperature dropped. By morning there was a coating of ice on everything. Tim had gotten an early call from the station and went in to deal with the chaos. There were a number of cars off the road and people were beginning to lose electricity. With the loss of power, alarm systems were going off all over town. It was going to be a nightmare for the police.

I was scheduled to have lunch with Alex Tate, but it would be suicide to travel in this weather. I called and left a message with his service. I knew New Hampshire was having the same ice storm we were having; still I was disappointed with having to cancel. Alex and I met for lunch several times a year. Before I moved to Maine it was more often, as he lived in Concord and I lived in Manchester. The two New Hampshire cities were only about seventeen miles apart. Today we had planned to meet in Portsmouth for lunch, but it wasn't going to happen.

I had the weather radio on to listen to weather updates. The ice storm was getting worse. By 10:00 a.m. over 400,000 home were without electricity in Maine and New Hampshire. I went to the storm cupboard and got out oil lamps and candles. From experience I knew it would be just a matter of time as the lights had already dimmed several times.

Around noon Tim called to tell me how crazy it was out there. The police were writing fender-bender reports and receiving reports of downed power lines.

"Don't even think about going out!" he said.

"My car is in the garage and I made a fire. I have no reason to go out. What about you?"

"I've got all the officers working, today. The Maine Turnpike is closed, and the governor has asked everyone to stay home. If I swing by later can you feed me?"

"Of course! Did Jessica get back to the university okay?"

"Yes, she left yesterday before the storm. I called her the first thing when I got into the office. She's safe and sound."

"At least as safe as anyone can be at a college these days."

"Thank you for that image. See you later!"

When I hung up, Argus looked up at me from his place by the fire. He heard the wind and the sleet hitting the window and put his head back down and drifted off to sleep again.

"Nice try Argus! Time to go out!"

Argus opened his eyes and then closed them again. Selective hearing! I went over and picked him up and took him to the backyard. He ran out to the middle of the yard and did his business and rushed back to me. We went back into the house.

In the time we had spent outside, the electricity had gone out. You never realize how much background noise there is in a house until the electricity dies. I lit the oil lamps and stoked the fire. The phone rang. It always surprises me that the phone never goes out, but the electricity often does. Aren't they on the same pole?

"Hey Jesse! Looks like lunch is off for today." It was Alex calling me back.

"Doesn't look good for the next few days either," I answered. "The power is out here."

"Most of southern New Hampshire is without power, too. I heard on the radio that this storm goes all the way to Quebec. I still have power at home, though."

"You're lucky. I have city water and a woodstove,

plus a gas range, so I should be okay for a day or too."

"Is Tim out working?"

"Oh, yes. He said it's crazy out there. The roads are icy and it's like bumper cars on the streets."

"Lunch next Monday?" he asked.

"Noon at the Whalers' Inn! I'll be there!"

Chapter 32

The storm had passed and the sun was out. The ice storm had left a beautiful glass-like coating on the trees and just about everything else. It was the worst ice-storm to hit the northeast in over a hundred years. We were told not to expect the power to be restored anytime soon. The power companies were very vague on the timeline for repairs, but they had crews out working twenty-four hours a day. Whole towns and cities were without power. No traffic lights, no street lights, and only places with emergency generators were open. TV stations had preempted regular programming to devote time to the storm. The only problem with that, of course, is that only people with power could watch it.

By the second day, the novelty had worn off. It wasn't bad during the day when there was sunlight, but oil lamps, propane lanterns, and candles don't give off enough light for reading. Tim was out straight at the police station and had only managed to come by twice for an impromptu meal.

The storm had pushed the Riley case to the bottom of Tim's list of things to do. He hadn't had time to question Billy Simpson about Harry Kahill's statement that he saw Billy heading toward the choir room prior to the murder. I decided to take it upon myself to talk to Billy. I did not for one minute think Billy Simpson could murder anyone. Still, the human heart is a mystery.

The middle school gym had been open as an emergency

shelter for three days. Many people were unprepared for the power outage and had taken refuge at the school. Rhonda and Jackson had power because they lived near downtown, which still had electricity. Jason and Monica had a generator they were using, and Viola went to stay with her sister in Portland. Billy Simpson had no heat and was staying at the school's emergency shelter. When I found that out, I drove over and picked him up.

The temperature had dropped and the specter of frozen pipes was on everyone's mind. After the storm it became apparent how much damage had been done. Metal transmission towers had buckled under the weight of the ice. Trees had broken off and damaged homes and automobiles. Home owners who relied on electricity to power their water pumps could not flush their toilets. I was lucky; the wood stove kept me warm, the gas stove allowed me to cook, and I had hot water from the propane water heater, so I could take a shower.

"Thanks for rescuing me," said Billy as he climbed into the Prius. Argus was jumping with excitement in the back seat.

"How bad is it there?" I asked.

"It's not bad. Everyone is in the same boat and people are really nice. But it's very boring. And there's been no news about when the power will be back on."

"According to the radio, it could take as long as a week. They are still finding more and more places where the lines have been totally destroyed and they have to string new ones."

"Well, thanks for offering me your guest room."

"No problem," I said. I didn't tell him I had brought him here to interrogate him about Jack Riley. The roads were mostly clear now, thanks to the salt trucks. We pulled up in front of Eagle's Nest and went carefully up the walkway.

"I've seen Tim a few times. He's been checking on the elderly and bringing them to the shelter," said Billy as we sat down by the fire with some hot coffee.

"This storm is especially hard on them. I imagine they are reluctant to leave home."

"Yes, they are. Many of them didn't realize they could bring their dogs to the shelter. So when Tim told them they could, they were eager to come. Many of them were very cold! I listened to quite a few of them while I was there." Billy looked around the room. "It seems nice and warm here

"Yes, the only damage I'll have will be the freezer. If the power doesn't return soon, I'll have to throw everything out. What a waste! Go settle yourself in the guest room and I'll get us something to eat."

I took some baked beans out of the refrigerator and put together a pan of cornbread. I was beginning to notice how much I relied on small kitchen appliances. Cooking required more thought when I didn't have a microwave or an electric mixer. I called Tim and told him I had picked up Billy.

"I'll try to come over later. Just be careful. If Billy is

the killer, then he could be dangerous, warned Tim.

"You think Billy is dangerous?" I asked.

"Not really. Just be careful."

Billy seemed eager to talk. I think his time at the shelter had been spent listening to other people's complaints.

"How did you hookup with Jack Riley? He wasn't all that likeable."

"I had to deliver a report to the standing committee at church. I was the head usher and it was my turn to be present. We started talking during the break and hit it off. He was actually quite nice when he wasn't in charge of anything." Jack Riley being nice didn't seem to be credible.

"Really?" I asked. "So how did you happen to go to Lake Placid with him?"

"He invited me, so I thought 'what the heck.'"

"Were you two serious about a relationship?"

"No, it was just for kicks." I couldn't imagine getting any kicks from Jack Riley. Billy must have been more than half in the bag at the time.

"Okay, I better level with you." I told him about Harry Kahill's report that he saw Billy heading toward the choir room on the day Jack died.

"I never went near the choir room. I was on duty and in the church the whole time. The last time I saw Jack Riley was when he took the collection plate and left the service."

"And you never left the sanctuary?"

"Not until the end of the service, and then I went

home. Is Harry sure it was me?"

"He said he *thought* it was you," I answered.

"Why did he wait so long to say anything?" asked Billy. It was a good question, but the phone rang before I could give any time to the question. It was Tim calling back.

"Everything okay over there?" Tim asked.

"Fine here, how about you?"

"Someone just reported a dead body. I'll be working later than I thought."

"Hypothermia?" I asked.

"Murder," replied Tim. "The bible thumper, the one you saw on the night where you fell on the ice was found slumped in the back doorway of Erebus!"

Billy, Tim, and I had a late dinner and then turned in early. Tim had questioned Billy, but came up with the same answers as I had earlier. Neither of us believed that Billy could be involved, but we still had to ask.

It was the third day without power and people were beginning to panic. The storm had caused millions of dollars in damages. The mail, however, continued to arrive. Mostly bills but one package did arrive that I had been waiting for. A copy of my new book, *The Bohemian Cookbook*, had arrived. I was relieved to see that my picture did not appear on the cover. When I wrote my first cookbook, I had been duped to dress as white trash and photographed on the steps of a trailer. This time there were illustrations by an artist. There was, however, one review printed on the inside that referred to me as "The White Trash Cook." Oh, well.

"That your new book?" asked Billy. I passed it to him. "Cool!"

"What are you up to today?" I asked.

"I'm going to my house and see what the damage is. Maybe the power will be back on there. What about you?"

"I'm going into Erebus to work. The store has power and I'm tired of sitting in the dark. I'll leave the back door unlocked so you can get in if you still have no power."

There was yellow police tape around the back door of Erebus, so I entered through the front door. Rhonda was already there. Today she was dressed in a fifties style dress that looked like she had just stripped it off Donna Reed. The shop was brightly lit, and it was wonderful to return to something like a normal life. I began to have a real appreciation for my forebears who lived in more primitive conditions.

"You're lucky you didn't lose power," I told her. "It sucks and I'm better off than most."

"I'm very lucky. Everyone who has come in has had a horror story to tell. I think if the power isn't restored soon, there is going to be a revolution!"

"Count me in for that," I said.

"So what's with the body out back?" I asked.

"I don't know. We were closed for two days. Someone found him slumped in the doorway when they went to the parking lot. They called the police. I didn't know anything about it until Tim called. What do you know?"

"Tim thinks the cause of death was a blow to the head, but it not official until the coroner checks it out. The police are trying to ID him now. Where's Mary sunshine?" I asked referring to Viola.

"She's still at her sister's house and said she's not coming back until the power come back on."

"If I hear 'Bright Blessings' one more time you might find her slumped in the back doorway," I said.

"My, my! Someone is grumpy today. What's up?"

"Nothing really. Billy Simpson is staying at Eagle's Nest, and Tim's been working about twenty hours a day." I went on to tell her about Billy being a 'person of interest' in the Jack Riley case. "The problem is, I know Billy didn't do it, but I don't have a clue who did."

"Do you think it will ever be solved," asked Rhonda.

"No," I replied. "None of it makes any sense." I was wrong, of course. It all made perfect sense when several days later I discovered one piece of information that made the whole thing clear!

Chapter 33

The power on Sagamore Street came back on the fourth day after the storm. Billy had his power restored the day before and had returned home. I was sitting by the fire when the lights flickered and then came on. At the same time the radio, TV, furnace, and the refrigerator all came to life with a lot of noise. I turned off the radio and TV and reset all the digital clocks that were flashing 12:00. I turned on every light in the living room and kitchen, just to enjoy a respite from the darkness and shadows.

Tim had been able to stay overnight and was sleeping late, but the sudden return to the twenty-first century woke him up. I passed him a cup of coffee as he entered the living room.

"It's about time," he said. "At least some people will be able to leave the shelter."

"Maybe your job will return to normal, and I can see you once in a while."

"This pretty much puts the stamp on my retirement papers. I wasn't looking forward to retirement, but this has changed my mind. June first and I'm done!"

"Great news! Do you have to go into work this morning?" I asked.

"I'm phoning it in right after breakfast. Get dressed and I'll take you to Ruby's."

Ruby's restaurant was crowded. A lot of people had electric stoves and couldn't cook even if they had heat in their houses. A table was found, as it usually was, for the chief of police. Officer Janet Murphy joined us for breakfast to give Tim an update.

"The body has been identified as Daniel Weston from Freeport, age thirty-eight. His family has been contacted and identification made. He has been in and out of mental facilities for the last four years. He had been making good progress, but the doctor took him off his medication, and he began acting out and then disappeared." Janet had ordered a fruit plate with cottage cheese. It didn't look like a breakfast to me.

"Do they know why the doctor took him off medication?" I asked.

"No, though it's common practice in some cases to take a person off medication before starting new ones," replied Janet.

"And the official cause of death?" asked Tim.

"Just as you expected, chief. Cause of death was a blow to the back of the head."

"Was he killed by the back door of Erebus?" I asked.

"According to the coroner, he was probably killed somewhere else and positioned in the doorway," she answered.

"Why?" I asked.

"Good question!" replied Tim.

The Whalers' Inn was a modest restaurant on the waterfront of Portsmouth, New Hampshire. Alex Tate was already seated in a booth when I walked in. I waved as I crossed the room, we shook hands and I sat down.

"Any trouble getting here?" he asked.

"There was an accident on the Maine Turnpike that slowed me down a bit, but other than that, no problem."

"I came over route four, and you know what that's like," Alex said.

"Yes, I do. I remember when I lived in Nottingham and my neighbor had a bumper sticker that said 'Pray for Me, I drive Route 4.'"

Alex put the menu down. "Are you ordering your usual?"

"Lobster stew, of course," I replied. We had been eating here two or three times a year for the last several years, and I always ordered the same thing.

"I have to admit they make a great one here," agreed Alex.

"I wanted to ask you something," I began. "I don't know if you read about a murder we had back in the fall, but a guy named Jack Riley was murdered. Does that ring a bell?"

"No, should it?"

"He was involved with your organization, the South American Physician Volunteers, as a fund raiser. He worked with the group of fund raisers out of the Lake Placid office," I explained.

"No, I don't work with the finances at all. I'm the coordinator for the doctor volunteers."

And then when he answered my next question, all

the pieces of the puzzle fell into place. I must have been so blind not to have seen it! Not only did I now know who the killer was, but I also knew that this was a very dangerous individual! All I had to do now was prove it!

Snow was falling and the weather forecasters predicted somewhere between six and ten inches of snow. Even at this early hour, people were panicking and rushing to the supermarkets. I was up early and took Argus for a walk before the snow got too deep. Argus hates snow and doesn't like to get his paws wet, so an early walk was advisable. I had a busy day ahead of me, so I put Argus in his crate and headed downtown. It was too early to open Erebus, and I needed coffee badly.

The coffee shop was full and Brian Stillwater was behind the counter turning out lattes and espressos. There was a bag lady huddled in the corner. She was all bundled up, and at the next table I spotted Harry Kahill .

"Morning Harry, do you mind if I join you?" I asked.

"Good morning Jesse; have a seat."

"It's awfully late in the year to have the first major snow storm."

"Better snow than ice. The hospital was crazy during the power outage."

"I imagine it was bad," I replied. I took a swallow of coffee. I really needed a caffeine jolt.

"Anything new on the Riley case?" he asked. "I

hope I didn't get Billy in trouble. I just thought I should say something."

"Funny you should ask; there have been a few new developments. In fact I'm pretty sure we have the killer identified." I looked around the coffee shop. We were off in a corner and no one was paying much attention to us.

"Who is it? Anybody I know?"

"It's you Harry, or whatever your real name is!"

"You're crazy!" sputtered Harry, but the color drained from his face.

"The real Dr. Harry Kahill died in a remote village in Chile eight years ago. When you failed to diagnose Jack Riley in time to save his life, he looked into your background. I should have made the connection earlier when I saw the South American Physician Volunteers certificate on your wall. Jack was a fund raiser for the organization, and it didn't take him long to figure it out. He threatened to expose you, but his fatal mistake was to try and blackmail you."

"You think you're so smart!" Harry snarled. "You can never prove it!" Harry pushed the table toward me, picked up his chair, and threw it at me. I ducked out of the way, the chair just barely missing me. He ran for the door.

He moved quickly, but there was a sudden commotion and the bag lady was on top of him. She stuck her knee in his back and pulled his arms backward and handcuffed him. Officer Janet Murphy took off her wool cap and shook her blonde hair loose.

"Good job, Jesse! We got him!" She smiled up at me. She picked Harry up off the floor and read him his rights.

"Good job, Ashes!" said a man in a heavy parka from the other side of the room. It was Tim bundled up as a shipyard worker. "You might develop some useful skills after all."

"I already have some useful skills," I answered.

"Don't I know it!" came the reply with a wink.

Epilogue

The snow had been heavier than expected, and even though the days were getting longer, it wasn't really noticeable; it was already dark. It was late Sunday afternoon, and it seemed that everyone I knew was crowded into my kitchen. I was dishing out homemade tomato soup and Tim was grilling cheese sandwiches.

The account of the arrest of Harry Kahill in the local newspaper left out some important details and everyone wanted to know the real story. According to the *Times-Record*, the police were instrumental in tracking down Jack Riley's killer by careful police work. My part in the investigation and the information provided by my friend Alex Tate were not part of the official story. That was fine with me.

"So what is the real story?" asked Beth White as we all settled in the living room with our soup and sandwiches.

"Well," began Tim, "Jesse was the first to figure out that it was Harry Kahill. His friend, Alex, was a recruiter for the South American Physician Volunteers. When Jesse asked if he knew Harry Kahill, he answered that he did know him and was sorry that he died. When Jesse told me that, we showed Alex a picture of Harry Kahill, and he identified him as Henry Kilroy, a medic who worked for the real Harry Kahill in Chile. So when Harry Kahill died, Henry Kilroy assumed his identity and moved to Bath. Because the real Kahill was from San Francisco, he thought he would be safe here."

"He killed Jack Riley," I said, taking up the narrative, "When Jack threatened to expose him. Jack had figured out that Kilroy was not a real doctor when he failed to diagnose his cancer correctly. Jack had been, by the way, skimming off the church's collection for months, which is why he left early with the collection. Kilroy suspected Jack of ripping off the church and wanted to catch him.

"So how does everything else tie in with Harry Kahill, or whatever his name is?" asked Rhonda.

"James Foster, the guest minister who was supposed to preach in October did not fall and hit his head like we thought. Kilroy hit him. Remember that when we found him the good doctor was already there. Kilroy was afraid Foster knew the real Harry Kahill," explained Tim. "Once we captured him and took him to the station, he confessed to everything."

"He also was the one in the dark hooded sweatshirt who set fire to the church," I added. "He also slipped something into Tim's coffee to speed up his heart."

"Why?" asked Jason.

"He was trying to create distractions," added Tim. "We found out that he was also the doctor of Daniel Weston, the guy we found dead in the doorway of Erebus. He took him off his medication. Later he killed him and placed him in the doorway as a warning to Jesse and me."

"What about Jesse's head injury in the parking lot?" asked Monica.

Murder in the Choir Room

"That," said Tim with way too much pleasure, "was Jesse being clumsy. We can't blame Kilroy for that one!"

"Were you in danger when you faced him in the coffee shop?" asked Billy.

"Not at all," I answered. "There were at least three cops in the shop that morning."

"And you let him face this killer?" Monica turned to Tim.

"He's a big boy," answered Tim. "And it was practice for his new job."

"What new job?" asked Rhonda.

"That brings us to the part where we make our big announcement," said Tim. We had everyone's attention at this point.

"Okay everyone," I began. "Tim is taking over the B. G. Boyce Security and Investigation Agency when he retires, and I'm going to be working for him," I said.

"Looks like you'll have to find a replacement for Internet sales, Rhonda!" added Tim.

Jason offered a toast, "To the future of the B.G. Boyce Agency!"

"And speaking of the future," said Rhonda pointing to the chocolate cake on the buffet, "that sour cream chocolate cake better be in my immediate future!"

Stephen E. Stanley

Recipes from Jesse's Recipe Box.

Jesse has collected old church and community cookbooks from Maine for over twenty years. These old recipes come from a time when great food variety was limited. Maine cooks were creative and, with few ingredients, managed to feed their families. Many of these recipes contain higher levels of fat and sugar than today's diets dictate. Jesse has adapted many of these recipes, some which go back to colonial days, to reflect today's higher health consciousness.

Jesse has a few rules about ingredients.   In baking, always use real butter and real vanilla extract, never margarine or imitation vanilla. Use meat and chicken sparingly, and when you do use it, try to obtain farm-raised organic meat, or free range poultry. The higher cost will be offset by the better flavor, and you will be supporting small family farms, and not supporting the inhumane factory-farming agribusinesses.

Murder in the Choir Room

Main Dishes

American Chop Suey.

American Chop Suey is a dish created during the depression that continued to be a favorite during World War II when rationing was in effect. By the 1950's, is simplicity and cost made it one of America's most popular comfort foods. The recipe has many variations, but the basic ingredients are ground beef, elbow macaroni, and some type of tomato sauce. During war rationing, it was often made with sliced up hot dogs and tomato soup, as these sometimes were more readily available than ground beef and tomato sauce. Here is Jesse's version:

1 lb of ground beef
1 onion
1 box elbow macaroni
1 package of mushrooms
1 can tomato sauce
1 cup shredded cheese

1 green pepper
1 tsp red pepper flakes
1 tsp Italian seasoning
1 can diced tomatoes
¼ cup red wine

Chop up onion green pepper and mushrooms with red pepper flakes. Add ground beef and brown. Drain off grease and add tomato sauce, wine, and diced tomato. Simmer on low for 10 minutes. Boil macaroni according to directions. Drain macaroni and add sauce, top with cheese. Tofu can be used in place of beef to make a vegetarian version.

Stephen E. Stanley

Chicken in the Pan

This is a great recipe for an electric fry pan. It was originally a one-pot meal from colonial times.
4 boneless, skinless chicken breasts.
4 onions cut up
4 medium potatoes cut up
8 carrots, peeled and sliced
A handful of green beans, cut up (for color)
1 ½ cups chicken or vegetable stock.
Brown chicken in oil at 350 degrees. When brown add vegetables with the stock. Reduce heat to 250 and simmer until chicken and vegetables are done.

Crockpot Baked Beans

Beans are a traditional New England dinner for Saturday nights. Leftover beans are then served for breakfast.
2 cups of dry beans, cover with water and cook on top of the stove for ½ hour.   Drain and place in oiled crock pot. Add:

1 tsp salt	2 tbsp molasses
2 tsp dry mustard	1 medium onion cut up
2 tbsp ketchup	1 tbsp Worcestershire sauce
¼ cup olive oil	

Cover beans with vegetable stock and cook on low for 6-8 hours. Add stock or water as needed.

Murder in the Choir Room

Vegetable Pie

This is a tasty main dish for non meat eaters. A great way to use leftover vegetables.

1 cup cut-up, cooked asparagus (Other vegetables can be substituted.)

1 small onion diced	½ cup mushrooms
1 cup shredded cheddar cheese	1 ½ cups milk
¾ cup biscuit mix	3 eggs
1 tsp salt	

Mix all ingredients together, place in a greased pie plate and bake at 400 degrees for 35 minutes.

Stephen E. Stanley

Stifado (Greek Stew)

Jesse spent two summers backpacking through Greece and returned home with a love of Greek food. The aroma of this cooking will bring neighbors to your door.

3 lbs stew beef
½ cup butter
2 pounds peeled onions
1 (6 oz.) can tomato paste
½ cup red wine
2 tbsp wine vinegar

1 tbsp brown sugar
1 bay leaf
1/8 tsp ground cloves
1/8 tsp cinnamon
¼ tsp cumin
2 tbsp raisins

Cut beef into one-inch cubes. Season with salt and pepper. Melt butter in dutch oven. Add meat and onions. Mix tomato paste, wine vinegar, and brown sugar and pour over meat and onion. Add bay leaf, spices, and raisins to pot. Cover and simmer for 3 hours.

Crab and Corn Chowder.
Jesse always makes this in October to celebrate autumn.

1 lb fresh cooked crabmeat.
2 medium potatoes diced
½ cup chopped onion   3 ears of corn
1 small can of creamed corn   4 Tabs butter
1 cup half and half   1 cup milk
Salt and pepper
1 can condensed milk

Boil onion and potatoes until tender. In pot melt butter and
sauté crabmeat for 2 minutes. Steam corn and cut off of the
cob. Add potato, onion, and corn. Stir in milk and half and
half. Add creamed corn. Take off stove and place overnight
in refrigerator. Heat to serve.

Sour Cream Chocolate Cake

*Rhonda loves this cake! Jason and Monica requested it for
their wedding cake.*

1 egg   1 tsp soda
½ cup cocoa   ½ tsp salt
½ cup oil   1 tbsp vanilla
1 ½ cup flour   ½ cup sour cream
1 cup sugar   ½ cup hot coffee

Mix all ingredients together. Pour into a greased and floured
tube pan. Bake at 350 degree for 40-45 minutes. Finish with
a dusting of powdered sugar.

Stephen E. Stanley

Donut Muffins

2 cups flour	1 tsp soda
½ cup oil	½ tsp nutmeg
1 cup sugar	2 eggs
1 cup plain yogurt	1 tbsp vanilla

Bake in greased muffin pan in a 350 degree oven for 20 minutes. Brush tops with melted butter and dust with sugar and cinnamon mix.

Easy Biscuits
Jesse uses this recipe on busy days.

2 cups flour	3 tsp baking powder
½ tsp salt	¾ cup sour cream
½ tsp baking soda	1 tbsp cold water

Mix all ingredients. Add more water if needed. Form into a soft dough and shape or cut into biscuit. Bake at 450 degree for about 12 minutes.

Corn Bread.

There are two versions of cornbread: Southern and New England. Southern cornbread doesn't use sugar and New England cornbread does.

1 cup flour	1 cup corn meal
4 Tabs sugar	1 tbsp baking powder
½ tsp salt	2 eggs
1 cup sour cream	¼ cup oil
1 tbsp honey or molasses	

Mix all ingredients together. Bake at 425 degrees: 25 minutes for a 9 x 9 greased pan. 15 minutes for muffins.

Applesauce Muffins

1 ½ cups applesauce	1/3 cup brown sugar
1 cup whole wheat flour	1/3 cup melted butter
1 egg	1 tsp soda
½ tsp salt	1 tsp baking powder
1 ½ cup white flour	½ tsp cinnamon

Mix all ingredients together and bake in a 350 degree oven for 20 minutes.

Stephen E. Stanley

Blueberry Muffins

1 egg	1 ½ cup flour
½ cup plain yogurt	½ cup sugar
¼ cup oil	2 tsp baking powder
½ tsp salt	1 tbsp vanilla
1 cup blue berries (other berries can be substituted)	

Mix all ingredients together and bake in a greased muffin pan at 400 degrees for 20 minutes.

Cranberry Scones.

¼ cup shortening	¼ cup brown sugar
½ cup sugar	2 ½ cups flour
4 tsp baking soda	½ tsp salt

Cut above ingredients together. Then add:

1 cup milk	1 egg
1 tbsp vanilla	1/2 cup cranberries

Mix dough until soft, roll out and cut into wedges. Bake at 425 degrees for 15 minutes. Brush with a glaze with 2 tbsp of apricot jam and 1 tbsp of water.

Red Velvet Cake
There are many variations of the Urban Legend that go with this cake. Red Velvet Cake was a dessert created at the Waldorf-Astoria in New York City in the 1920's. According to the legend, a woman in 1930 asked for the recipe for the cake. She received the recipe and a bill for thirty dollars. Indignant, she spread the recipe in a chain letter.

2 ½ cups of flour	1 ½ cups of sugar
2 tsp cocoa	1 tsp soda
1 tsp salt	2 eggs
1 tbsp white vinegar	½ cup oil
1 cup plain yogurt	
¼ cup red food coloring (or 2 oz. bottle)	
1 tbsp vanilla	

Mix all ingredients together. Pour into three greased and floured 8-inch pans. Bake at 350 degrees for 30 minutes.

Frosting:

½ stick of butter	8 oz cream cheese
1 lb box powered sugar	1 tsp vanilla

Stephen E. Stanley

Made in the USA
Lexington, KY
12 February 2011